"Sheriff, stop them!"
Evans begged. "Make them stop!"

"Why, sure," Renwick replied with yawning disinterest. "Of course, a lynch mob is a powerful, terrible force to buck, me bein' one lone man against all these well-meanin' friends and neighbors."

Evans let out a tormented moan, his defiance showing signs of weakening. He looked around frenziedly, as though trying to see some way to escape, and saw only an encirclement of stony, merciless faces.

"Don't do it!" he pleaded. "Dead men can't talk."

Hodel chuckled. "Live ones who won't are as good as dead."

Jessie gave a soft, satisfied sigh as Evans began to talk.

Also in the LONE STAR series
from Jove

WESLEY ELLIS

LONE STAR

AND THE
GUNPOWDER CURE

A JOVE BOOK

LONE STAR AND THE GUNPOWDER CURE

A Jove Book/published by arrangement with
the author

PRINTING HISTORY
Jove edition/July 1986

ISBN: 0-515-08608-8

Jove Books are published by The Berkley Publishing Group,
200 Madison Avenue, New York, N.Y. 10016. The words
"A JOVE BOOK" and the "J" with sunburst are trademarks
belonging to Jove Publications, Inc.

PRINTED IN THE UNITED STATES OF AMERICA

LONE STAR

AND THE
GUNPOWDER CURE

Chapter 1

Abram Volner's burial was held near sundown when streaks of orange, pink, and lavender still highlighted the horizon.

Two wagons comprised the entire procession that rolled slowly along the main street of Elbow, Arizona Territory. Volner's funeral, like any funeral, stirred enough interest to cause the townsfolk to pause, crane their necks, and strain their eyes to study his passing cortege. But to them he was merely a name, an unknown outsider who'd arrived alive one morning and departed dead that night. And a stranger's funeral failed to stir enough interest for them to suffer heat and to endure sermons in order to watch his final interment. So the cortege, having left town, fell from mind as well as sight; alone, it crossed a wooden bridge over the dry Sangrar Wash, then traveled eastward through rosy vestiges of a torpid summer day to the remote, hillside cemetery.

The lead wagon, which was painted a dull black and had a fringed canopy over driver and bed, bore Volner's remains in a plain coffin. On the hearse's hard seat, the morose, cadaverously thin mortician held loose reins and allowed his two mares to pull at their own pace.

Alongside sat the local attorney, Quentin Pollard. He was in his fifties, bald, bejowled, and blustery by nature. He had a hint of swagger in the rake of his high-crowned bowler and in the immaculate press of his dark suit, which barely constrained his rotund build. He kept shifting impatiently, as if wishing the trip were over, but the only time he suggested they speed up, the mortician reminded him that haste would billow choking dust clouds back at the other wagon.

The wagon behind was a single-harness, open-ranch surrey driven by Reverend Sigismund Flynn. He was withered and frail and looked to be eighty. Yet he was still actively rooting out sloth and deviltry as Elbow's combination schoolmaster and preacher. Or so he claimed proudly to Jessica Starbuck and Ki, who were riding in the rear seat of his surrey.

The grave was located on a grassy knoll, the grass brown and parched now, the freshly shoveled earth resembling hard, chunky stone. When the wagons arrived, the two men hired as gravediggers were resting with their horses in the shade of a stunted tree. They scrambled to their feet as the mortician braked his hearse and helped him unload and carry the coffin to the open grave.

Reverend Flynn then began intoning several prayers and other tributes to the heavenly home to which he bequeathed Abram Volner's immortal soul. While he devoutly chanted on in his quavering voice, the men used ropes to lower the coffin, planting Volner with his head to the East, his feet to the West. The casket had been cloaked by a piece of black cloth, which fluttered in a faint, erratic breeze, as did the open pages of Reverend Flynn's Bible.

Jessie kept her expression somber; her cameo face impassive, betraying none of the emotions roiling beneath the surface. A sensuous lady in her mid-twenties, she did not appear to be especially wealthy, which she was, being sole heir to the international business empire founded by her late father, Alex Starbuck. She was clad in common range garb, worn and dusty from the sweaty ride she and Ki had just made from Tucson. Her taut, full breasts thrust tremulously against her tight blouse and denim jacket. Her pinned coils of long, coppery-blond hair were disheveled,

2

wisps floating in the light breeze as she stood, head bowed. Her eyes darkened almost to emerald. Her hand pressed her flat-crowned hat against the right thigh of her jeans, where normally she wore her custom Colt pistol. Out of respect, she had left her pistol and holster belt in her saddlebag; out of habit, she still carried her twin-shot derringer hidden behind her belt buckle.

Ki, dressed as he was in jeans, cotton-twill collarless shirt, old leather vest, and rope-soled slippers, did not seem to be much of anything—certainly not a threat, not a man to be reckoned with. Yet Ki, born to the Nipponese wife of an American sailor and then orphaned as a boy in Japan, had trained in martial arts and the deadly skills of a samurai; and while even now, in his early thirties, Ki refused to pack a firearm, his vest contained short daggers and other small throwing weapons, including the razor-sharp, star-shaped steel disks known as *shuriken*. When, years earlier, he'd first come to America, he'd placed his talents in the service of Alex Starbuck—indeed, he and Jessie had virtually grown up together, and after her father's murder, it proved fitting for him and Jessie to continue together, as affectionately bonded as any actual brother and sister could be. So, in concordance with Jessie, Ki looked stoic, his eyes and lean features concealing his actual mood behind a mask of outward dispassion.

Inwardly they both seethed with grim, agitated fury. They had never met Abram Volner; they just knew of him. Originally Volner was an enlisted trooper, rising to serve as adjutant and law clerk at numerous posts. He was honorably discharged at Fort Dodge. He then was hired by Starbuck as a field investigator and, if attorneys weren't needed, as a legal adjuster. Consistantly he asked for risky missions; evidently he'd always courted danger, living on the brink through the Civil War, several Indian campaigns, outlaw raids, railroad incursions, and finally trouble-shooting perils as a roving Starbuck operative. He survived

3

them all, only to be sent on a harmless minor task to a supposedly peaceful community, where he was promptly ambushed, robbed, and killed. And that's what galled Jessie and Ki. It was too bad an end for such a brave, loyal employee. Well, loyalty breeds loyalty, and somehow Starbuck would repay Abram Volner his full due.

"We therefore commit his body to the ground, earth to earth, ashes to ashes, dust to dust..." Reverend Flynn knelt as he read aloud, scooped up a handful of dirt, and sprinkled it into the grave. Nodding, he pocketed his Bible. "Close it up now, lads."

The diggers shoveled the earthern pile, and when they finished mounding the grave, they erected at its head a plain white cross. Pollard thanked the mortician, declared he'd return with Reverend Flynn, and then crossed to the surrey where the reverend was already at the reins and itching to leave. Jessie and Ki climbed in the back, while Pollard joined Reverend Flynn in front with a doleful, "Fine service, Preacher, fine service." Reverend Flynn wheeled his surrey around and headed into the dusk.

Nobody spoke for a while, save for the reverend crabbing at his horse, until Pollard cleared his throat and said, "Met your Mr. Volner briefly once, Miss Starbuck. A nice man, a sore loss to his family, though danged if we could locate his kin. Still, considering your coming, it's a shame he wasn't laid to rest in grander style."

"He was a bachelor with no known relatives," Jessie replied politely. "I'm sure he would've approved of his funeral. It was splendid, and I'm simply pleased we were able to arrive in time."

"How gratifying to hear," Reverend Flynn remarked. "Y'see, he was kept as long as possible, till the heat and nature of his demise made him, ah, ripe and necessitating a rapid Christian burial."

"He was waylaid, stabbed, and found a couple of miles

4

out on the north road," Pollard explained. "I was shocked. He told me when he visited that he was only going to rent a room. I still haven't an inkling why he happened to be riding way out there."

"Talk is that Frederick Tode knows," Reverend Flynn said.

"Ridiculous. Froggy loots fools at the gambling tables and makes more at it and in less time than he could by robbing. No more sense to it than to the rumors about him when Mr. Latimer upped and sickened. Froggy has nothing to gain by it," Pollard said and then regarded Jessie with thoughtful concern. "It occurs to me my comment about Froggy may apply to you. Are you aiming to carry out your plan?"

"Perhaps," she hedged. "I've nothing to gain if I do, but nothing to lose. If the Latimers gain by it, more power to them."

"Not doubting your motives, but your generous gift would be like those of a gent I knew who gave presents of hornets' nests."

"Meaning?"

"Meaning there's a feud brewing between the Box L ranch you inherited and the bordering dairy farm owned by Uriah Nehalem. Your sheep are at the core of it. Nehalem hates them with a passion, and having them next door has him frothing mad."

"Do the Latimers let the sheep stray or spoil range?"

Pollard shook his head. "The Box L is fenced, and best word is that the sheep are properly tended and don't do any harm. Years ago it was part of the dairy farm, but the land's lousy for cows. It has too many steep hills and too many rocks and holes. Nehalem sold it gladly, bragging of his shrewd deal till Thad Latimer brought in his sheep, which thrive like crazy there. Nehalem threw a fit, yet he'd done it to himself and couldn't change it legally."

5

"But Nehalem's apt to change it illegally, if I sign the Box L over to Latimer's sons and they continue to raise sheep, is that it?"

"That's my fear, yes, and more. Nehalem used to be a roughshod honcho hereabouts, but his popularity's slipping as old-timers make way for fresh blood. Plenty of newcomers are siding with the Latimers—some 'cause they know sheep can get along in cattle country and crowd out cattle, most 'cause they don't much like sheep but love sticking burrs under Nehalem's saddle. They're independent and feisty, eager to tangle over arguments. So what once began as a personal tiff has been steadily worsening, until recently there've been crew skirmishes, mainly brawls but a few gunfights. Some say Thad Latimer was shot by a Nehalem hand. I don't know. I don't know what possessed Latimer to will his Box L to you, Miss Starbuck. I do know your noble gift could well be the spark that ignites a range war."

"I see. Well, I'll think it over."

"Until when?"

"I'll think it over."

Pollard took a deep breath and managed a chuckle. "All right, I know better than to try to budge a lady. Let's leave it lie for now."

They let it lie, lapsing silent again. Jessie gazed out at the scenery as the wagon descended the hillside trail to Elbow, yet her thoughts kept returning to the Box L. Pollard's sketch of local problems she took seriously, for he was in a position to know, and it agreed with field operative reports she'd read weeks earlier. And it bothered her, just as this whole situation had been nagging at her like a thorn in her flesh.

Months ago, Jessie learned that Starbuck was inheriting the property of a sheeper. A record check indicated Thaddeus Latimer never had a connection with Starbuck. A cursory investigation disclosed he'd been a widower with sons

Glenn and Dwight, whom he'd cut from his will after a domestic spat. His reason for choosing Starbuck had gone with him to his grave; the best guess was that he'd had a nasty sense of humor and felt it funny to inflict a huge cattle organization with a sheep outfit. His thumb in the eye irked Jessie, but it had to be resolved. She instructed that as soon as the Box L was officially Starbuck's, it should be deeded to Glenn and Dwight, who rightfully deserved it.

Eight days ago, the Box L cleared probate. As per her orders, Volner was dispatched to Elbow to arrange the deed's transfer. That should have been the finish of it. Instead, it was the finish of Volner.

The news of his murder and imminent burial reached Jessie at Tucson, when she and Ki left the train to check for messages in the depot. She could've turned the murder over to an operative and continued on her trip back to her Circle Star ranch in Texas. But the gravity of homocide and of a potential feud and her nettling intuition of worse yet to come convinced her to go personally. And go quickly. With luck, Volner would have two mourners at his funeral.

Renting horses was out, since liveries insisted they be returned in short order. So after some careful searching, Jessie haggled the buy of a rambunctious roan gelding and a deep-brisketed mare pinto and accompanying gear. For two days she and Ki beat steadily over trails to the Sangrar Wash. There they dipped south, flanking the wash down through Rainbow Valley until they arrived in Elbow, where they drew rein.

Despite their condition, Jessie felt impelled to call on Quentin Pollard, whom she knew had been Volner's contact here. A fortunate choice: If they'd delayed fifteen minutes, they'd have missed him and the burial. Having no time, they went as they were, sweaty and layered with gray dust, red dust, and other shades of dry, eroded dirt. They did take time for their weary horses, stabling them in the town's small livery before rejoining Pollard and meeting Reverend Flynn and the mortician at the funeral parlor.

Now the funeral was over, the tribute was done, and Jessie stared pensively at the land wherein Volner was laid.

The cemetery stood among foothills, and when the trail broke out across a sweeping ledge, Jessie was able to scan the surrounding vista of mountain and plateau. The foothills rose like jumbled steps to the tawny-peaked Sierra Estrellas, the range being the eastern limit of Rainbow Valley. Westward was a similar boundary, the dark slopes of the Maricopas. Waning sunset smeared their rimline, illuminating the valley floor that stretched, scalloped and corrugated, between the two ranges. Though Elbow itself was temporarily hidden by a ridge shoulder, Jessie could see dots of grazing cattle and faint smoke patterns from chimneys of scattered ranches. Edging the northern sky were clouds. Portents of rain, a rarity hereabouts, Jessie surmised—probably a weak drizzle or perhaps a brief summer storm, if anything at all.

The trail dipped from the ridge, which was petering out, and curved to avoid the ridge shoulder. Soon Elbow came into view, the last rays of sun glinting off the town's roofs and windows.

Elbow was shrouded by dusk when they arrived, its windows now aglow with lamplight. Lanterns hung along the main street, which was lined with typical storefront buildings, a law office and a jail, and noisy saloons. The street was clogged, the walks were packed, and the bars and open shops were enjoying a brisk trade.

At midtown, Reverend Flynn eased his surrey past the congested front of a large, two-story white building. It was the town's largest and its busiest, lively with people jostling one another to get in or out, mostly in. The sign across its overhang read: CASTLE DOME HOTEL & EATERY: GENTLEMANS CLUB—LADEYS WELCOME. Pollard highly recommended the hotel to Jessie and Ki, boasting it was the

8

gathering point for the best of Rainbow Valley. Anyway, it was the only hotel.

A block after, Reverend Flynn stopped to let his riders off at Pollard's office, which was in a modest, false-fronted structure that also housed a workshop area and his private quarters in back. Lettered on the darkened window was RAINBOW REGISTER, then, JOB PRINTING TO ORDER, and last, COUNSELOR QUENTIN S. POLLARD, PROP. It wasn't surprising that Pollard plied two trades; out in such an isolated area as this, he'd have starved trying to do only law work.

Jessie and Ki again thanked Reverend Flynn, Jessie adding as a casual farewell, "And my, your town seems remarkably crowded."

"Day's done and so's the sun. Evening brings them in." With a pleasant nod and a parting, "God bless," the preacher drove on.

"Evening and Doc Augustas bring them in," Pollard said, patting his pockets as if hunting for his door key. "Evening's when he opens his town clinic, and patients swarm from everywhere to see him. Like the hotel, he's tops and the only one here." Instead of a key, Pollard discovered a couple of pamplets, which he gave to Jessie and Ki. "Printed them myself. Tells about the health farm he runs."

The pamphlets looked stately with their scrolls and fretwork. The copy read: Ailing? Frail? Impotent? Attend Dr. Byron Augustas' Sanatorium, and discover new joy to life and the Fountain of Youth!

"Doc Augustas is a crack specialist at everything," Pollard continued, still without his key, but now having drawn from another pocket a thin, amber glass bottle. "He mixed this special for my catarrh." Pollard took a satisfying swig. "His place has a choice setting, always had, but only a wizard like him could recognize that all the sulphur pools there aren't stinkholes, but therapy cures."

Inside the pamphlets had the same florid style: Dr. Au-

9

gustas, renowned physician of Famous Personages and Crowned Heads of Europe... Practice now available to sufferers of any class... Bask in restorative dry sunshine, bathe in curative hot springs, heal with strengthening rare minerals and energizing medicinal herbs... Excellent cuisine, cabins, and private rooms... Write for rates and directions.

"We're darn lucky Doc moved here last year for his health and then decided to stay when Widow Kessler agreed to sell him the place. Hard on her, though. She found her husband one dawn slumped against the outhouse door with a bullet in his back. Froggy Tode got blamed for that killing, too, though he'd only been in town a week then. Baseless charge, of course, but it does go to show our state of nerves. Rubbed raw. Alarmed." Pollard recorked his bottle and, while stowing it away, located his key. "Think over my advice to you earlier, Miss Starbuck. Consider the consequences if you insist on giving the Box L to sheepers rather than, say, selling it to others. Then get back to me soon as possible. Well, I bid y'all good night."

After leaving Pollard, Jessie and Ki walked back toward the Castle Dome. "I sense this mess is already at a head," Ki said, "and we need to be fast in figuring how to cool it before it boils over."

Jessie nodded. "We certainly arrived with no time to spare. It's too dark and late to find the Box L tonight, but first light tomorrow, we'll get directions and ride out to see the Latimers."

The Castle Dome Hotel's lobby was mobbed, as were the eatery and gentlemen's club. Jessie and Ki managed to press in and rent rooms, however, with bath privileges down the hall. Then they pushed to the restaurant, where they waited long for a table and longer for their orders. They spent the time observing the horde around them and in the saloon, which was nearby through an open connecting door. The patrons were a mingle of ages and types, mostly ranchers and hands and the ilk, but some wore garb of the cities east of the Missouri. The restaurant had waiters who wore black tie. The saloon was more boisterous and smoky. Bartenders poured at the thronged counter, and girls in vivid décolleté dresses prowled the packed tables and games at the rear.

Eventually the waiter came with their food. As he was serving, a raucous laugh burst from the saloon, drawing their attention.

A stocky old man, they saw, had risen from a poker table and was strutting to the bar. "Give Mr. Tode a drink," he crowed loudly. "Hell, give a round to all them idiot cardsharps there. It's on me, but they been paying for it."

"Uriah Nehalem, owner of the biggest spread in the valley," the waiter remarked. "He's liable to hooraw when he wins good. Can't fault him. His wins are few and far between."

They eyed the man with keener interest. Nehalem had enormous shoulders, a square, lined face dominated by hard, gray eyes, and a brushy mustache. Especially they noted the length of his dangling arms, his assured manner, and the way his .44 Smith & Wesson single-action was holstered against his thigh.

The waiter left and they began eating, still watching the rough dairyman carry on in the saloon. When his drinks were served, he mockingly toasted the surly and unresponsive losers, only one of whom raised his glass in a return salute. That one had to be Frederick "Froggy" Tode, for he wore a gambler's black coat and snowy shirt, and he downright resembled a frog.

Nehalem downed his drink and shoved his glass over for another. While the bartender poured it, there was a stir at the saloon's street entrance, the doors swinging wide to admit a tall, muscular man of about thirty years. Clad in rangewear, he wore a heavy Colt on the left side, cross-drawn fashion, butt forward. Fine-featured, he had an aq-

11

uiline nose and prominent cheekbones. His battered
Stetson was tipped over one glittering brown eye, and his
devil-may-care bearing caused Jessie to associate him with
ruckus raising in general.

The waiter, who'd returned with coffee, started to
speak, and then gulped. "Gawshalmighty, it's Glenn Latimer. Here comes trouble."

Evidently those in the saloon thought so, too, shifting
stiffly aside as Latimer approached the bar. Nehalem
caught sight and seemed to swell slightly, his mustache
bristling, his right hand gliding down and hooking thumb
over his cartridge belt.

Latimer was almost to the bar before he became aware
of Nehalem in the crush there. He halted and stared, his
mouth slowly curving in a derisive grin. The effect appeared to madden Nehalem. His face darkened, and his
hand suddenly dropped toward his holster.

Latimer's hand slid across his middle at the same instant. The saloon grew intensely still, save for a shuffling
of bodies as the bartenders ducked and the others covertly
stepped out of line. The waiter serving Jessie and Ki set
their coffee down and scurried off to help customers at the
far end of the restaurant.

There was grim tragedy in the making.

Chapter 2

The stillness stretched thin and taut, too strained to hold for long. The two men were poised and ready for the break, each determined and wary of the other, locked in a feud concerning cows and sheep that now had become a personal animosity.

It was Nehalem who broke the unendurable hush, belligerently snapping, "What d'you figure this'll getcha, waltzing in here?"

"A drink," Latimer replied evenly. "Any objections?"

"You betcha! This's a respectable joint for decent citizens, and it don't cater to sheepers." In his ire, Nehalem fisted his gunhand and shook it menacingly. "So waltz back out of here."

Latimer gave a scoffing laugh and let his hand relax away from his revolver. "Since when do I dance to your say-so?"

"You'd better—while you can on your own feet. Don't stop till you're clear of our valley, and be sure to take your whelp of a kid brother along with you. I'm fed to the teeth with him bleatin' at my daughters like some two-legged lovesick sheep."

"Now get this straight." Latimer's voice was clipped, his lips peeled and revealing his teeth. There was a boxer's sag to his shoulders, and his hands kept flexing as if eager to squeeze something. "I'm not partial to moving once I'm rooted, so you're stuck with me staying. Besides, if I'm not proper enough for here, you sure's hell are not. I will

13

talk to Dwight for you, though. I'd prefer he spark a real ewe, anyway, to either of your daughters."

Goaded to sputtering, Nehalem moved swiftly for one his age. His long arms reached out, one hand seizing Latimer by the throat of his shirt, the other pistoning in a short, looping punch.

Latimer tried to wrench loose and dodge aside: a futile struggle. The fist struck the high edge of his jaw and snapped his head at an angle as if he'd hit the end of a hangman's noose. Nehalem then freed the shirt with a shove, and Lattimer staggered back against the bar, knocking it and toppling bottles. He grasped the counter to steady himself, satisfied for a moment just to suck what breath he could through his bruised throat.

"Strong-arming and shirt ripping's your style, eh?"

"For sheepers, it is."

Muscles tensing, Latimer sprang at Nehalem. The impact jarred the floor around them, and Nehalem's blow to the plexus jolted the air out of Latimer. The solid weight of Latimer's body, though, sent Nehalem backward in short steps to keep his footing until he could roll aside. Latimer pursued, tucking his chin and boring in with sledgehammering fists.

Nehalem moved forward to counter, coming in close and sending a smashing right into Latimer's nose, bringing a spurt of blood. Latimer snuffled and reflexively daubed the blood with his fingers, inadvertently lowering his guard and allowing Nehalem to catch him behind the ear with a great roundhouse swing. With his head twisting around and his legs stumbling awry, he was trying to regain his balance, but Nehalem locked fingers behind his neck and pivoted him into a waiting uppercut.

Latimer lost his footing, again reeling back. This time the bar rail broke his fall and saved him from smacking the floor. He sagged, using the rail for support as he recovered his wind and wits.

"Get out." Nehalem stood smugly, arms akimbo. "Keep out."

Latimer slowly groped upright. "Nuts. I'm sticking."

"You're leaving for good. Hell, you've no place to stay."

"The Box L," Latimer argued. "It's me'n Dwight's."

"Tell that to Starbuck when they come to sweep you and your sheep off it. See if the richest cattle company gives two ragtag sheepers a free ride. What a cackle! Betcha your dad cackled. He did to my face after bum steering me on buying the ranch for sheep—which's tame to how he fleeced you, his own sons."

Latimer stiffened, scowling. "Don't say such again."

Nehalem glanced to grin at a nearby bartender. "Acts like he's a landowner here, doesn't he? Like he wasn't gypped of his inheri—"

Latimer slapped Nehalem hard across the mouth with the flat of his hand, and the sound cracked like a pistol shot. "I told you to be careful how you talk," Latimer said coldly.

The slap was worse than a punch; it was an insult. Outraged, Nehalem wavered indecisive for a second, half pawing for his revolver before lunging forward to clutch Latimer by the throat again.

But Latimer was alert for this now and already was ducking, sidestepping, and crunching Nehalem in the chops. He pressed his advantage with a relentless compulsion, and Nehalem, thrown on the defensive, lashed back with a pummeling to body and head.

By now, the patrons were starting to cluster. The bartenders and night managers were gearing to intervene. And from their nearby table, Jessie and Ki were keeping watch on developments.

Ki was enjoying the fight to a degree, being mildly entertained by fast and fair matches, which this was. But mostly he was judging with an objective eye. The men were of similar height and weight, with Latimer having youth and Nehalem having experience. Speed was a toss-up, perhaps settled only by a duel, which made Ki wonder if Latimer had mastered the difficult yet extremely fast cross-draw pull.

Jessie was viewing them with mounting anxiety and exasperation. She read the implacable purpose in Latimer's features and the desperate fury in Nehalem's expression. She exclaimed, "Those clods! They've twice verged on shooting and'll end it that way yet if they don't beat themselves to death first. And look at those moping bartenders; they won't interfere. They don't want to get beaten silly."

"All right, Jessie, I'll see what I can do."

"Thanks, Ki. I wouldn't ask, but I do want both bums alive. And I want them on our side, to work with us, so don't just go flatten them. Don't hold back and get yourself beaten silly, either."

"Exactly what I like, easy instructions." Grinning lightly at Jessie with more assurance than he felt, Ki ambled into the saloon.

The two combatants were oblivious to Ki's casual approach. Nehalem was absorbed in blunting Latimer's savage attack, and Latimer was concentrating on increasing pressure and momentum. He couldn't have stopped himself if he'd wanted to, his fists slugging Nehalem's face, ribs, and belly with all the driving power in his muscles. Nehalem's head bounced backward at every brutal contact, and every time it tipped forward, Latimer's fist met it.

The impact of the incessantly battering one-two combinations drained the stamina from Nehalem's knees. He foundered, bumped against a saloon chair, lifted it, and hurled it with sudden strength.

Latimer bent, letting it cut the air over his back. He set his heels then, uncoiled with his right fist, launching it with all the force of his body behind it, and caught Nehalem on the chin.

Propelled some feet away from the bar, Nehalem wobbled on buckling legs, made a lurch for a nearby post, and lost his balance. He dropped abruptly and ungainly, almost smacking a big brass spittoon at the post's base. He landed square on his butt in a spraddle-legged position and sat dazed but far from out.

Ki, having worked to the front of the gathering, hoped the fight was over. Nehalem rolled, pushed to a crouch, wiped his lips, saw blood on his sleeve, and scowled belligerently at Latimer. Latimer stood breathing raspily through his mouth, but he was eyeing Nehalem with sardonic challenge. The fight wasn't over, Ki realized; this was but a momentary lull. Ki began sauntering toward Nehalem, picking him because he was nearer and was close to a spittoon.

Nehalem reared up, blood drooling from the corners of his lips. He swabbed them again. "I'll get you for this, sheeper."

"Get me now while I'm handy."

"I ought've shot you the first time I saw you," Nehalem snarled as he set his draw stance, unaware that Ki was moseying in by the post next to him. "Chances are I will, sooner or later."

"No, you won't!" Latimer hovered his hand over his revolver. "When you pull, I'll be facing you. Not like when my pa got it."

The words shook Nehalem, their insinuated charge causing his face to redden, his fingers to squirm in the palm of his gunhand.

Ki was now sidling between Nehalem and the post. Suddenly he tripped and caromed against the post, his foot kicking the brass spittoon and knocking it over. He swung, teetering, and his other foot came down awkwardly on the rounded surface. The spittoon rolled. Ki blundered wildly, windmilling his arms and grabbing for anything that would prevent him from falling.

The only thing within reach was Uriah Nehalem, who was raging at Latimer. "A slimy lie! Don't call me a back-shooting—yoiks!"

Nehalem reeled, startled. He careened from the unexpected cannonball of a body and struggled against the throttling wrap of arms and legs. He tried valiantly to recover his footing, but the spittoon became embroiled, and no manner of unwrangling could wrench loose the octopus squeeze of clinging limbs. Another second and Nehalem, Ki, and the bouncing spittoon crashed to the floor, all tangled together in a thudding, clanging heap.

Ki was on his feet first. He reached with his left hand, gripped the bellowing Nehalem by the shoulder, and helped him up.

"Sorry. I'm very sorry." Ki apologized abjectly to the swearing man, ignoring the ripple of surprised chatter and chuckles coming from the onlookers. "I didn't mean to upend you, sir, I was just trying to keep from falling. And thanks, because the way I was going down, I had a good chance of breaking something."

"You mighty nigh broke my neck!" Nehalem roared, then choked, his outbursts only fueling Latimer's laughter. "It's okay. Accidents can happen, and I don't want a feller to get hurt."

"Mighty understanding of you," Ki said, brushing dust off Nehalem's shirt. Peripherally he saw Latimer, grinning broadly and wiping tears, turn and start to stroll out of the saloon.

Nehalem suddenly seemed to recall his presence and glanced about, spotting him. "Time to git, huh, afore you hafta face me!"

Latimer pivoted, sobering. "I don't scare that easy," he retorted. "Had time for one drink, and time's about up. Besides, nothing could beat your show. You make a great mattress." His lips twitched into a smile; then he began to chortle. "Another time. I can't look at you and keep a

18

straight face." He swiveled and lumbered out of the door, doubled over in hearty guffaws.

Nehalem spluttered profanely. He was ignored, the saloon reviving with a sudden release from the tension—patrons returning to drinks, bartenders rattling bottles. Casting Ki a last peevish look, he stomped away, muttering to the bar. He yelled for service, "A double whiskey! I need a stiff nightcap before heading home."

Ki, turning to leave, noticed that Nehalem's shout seemed to interest two rough men. He hesitated, unsure, and watched the men chug their drinks and hasten toward the door. Then he moved on to the restaurant as they left, curious but unconvinced he'd spotted anything at all significant.

The table was empty. Figuring Jessie had most likely gone after Glenn Latimer, Ki sat down to wait. Shortly the manager came over, introduced himself, and profusely thanked Ki.

"I sure owe you one for stopping a ruckus," the manager said. "Saw your stunt once at a circus, where this clown fell on a toothpick so slickly, you'd swear he really did stumble over it."

Ki received a drink on the house. Pretty soon he glimpsed Nehalem leaving, and right after, Jessie showed up and joined him.

She looked harried. "Quick thinking, Ki, and it worked like a charm. Wish I'd been as quick catching Latimer as he left, but I missed and can't find him or a Box L horse along the street. A clerk told me, though, he's expected to pick his purchases up before going home, so he still should be around town."

"Well, let's check the livery. He may've stabled his horse."

Once outside, they turned toward the small livery at the edge of town. They walked briskly and kept alert for Latimer, Jessie again marveling how busy Elbow was for a rural town, and wondering if it was due to Dr. Augustas' sanatorium.

However, they saw nothing of Latimer. Finally they passed from the business section of the main street to where there were no more lanterns on poles and precious little activity. Beyond, the only illumination came from the moon and from lamplit windows, and the only person in direct view was a man moving slowly up ahead. They couldn't see his face, the man neglecting to turn or glance behind. But as their faster pace drew them nearer, Ki managed to recognize the blocky shape of Uriah Nehalem.

Almost immediately Nehalem vanished, cutting into the lane that led to the livery, which Jessie and Ki reached moments later. The lane ran a stretch before ending at the barn and corral, and it was flanked by adobes and shacks that mostly were dark and silent, although an occasional glimmering window and muffled hum of voices denoted occupancy. From the street corner, they glimpsed Nehalem about midway along the otherwise deserted lane, his head bent. He was apparently absorbed in thought and oblivious to danger.

Then, as he was passing the mouth of a slim pathway between two dwellings, something or somebody caused Nehalem to stop short and peer into the black entry. The next instant Jessie and Ki saw him rear as if bitten. "Whaddyuh mean, you want my roll?"

Faintly they heard the angry demand: "Yeah, fork it over."

"Why, cuss yuh! I won it fair'n square in a game, boys."

Jessie and Ki were hurrying, closing quietly, pressing to the dark of walls. Obviously Nehalem was under gun, and they feared an alarmed uproar would cause the robbers to fire before fleeing. The harsh voices of outrage and threat grew louder in their ears.

"C'mon, cough up the cash, or we'll blow you to smith-ereens!"

"Awri'! Awri'! Here, take it." Nehalem fumbled to remove a thick wad of currency from underneath his shirt. A robber stepped impatiently out of the concealing pathway, and despite his masked face, Ki identified him as one of the two he'd seen leave the saloon. The man snatched the money and backed a pace, thumbing to cock the hammer of his leveled revolver. Abruptly Nehalem realized he was to be killed to cover their crime. "No! Don't—"

The revolver discharged with lurid flame. Nehalem screamed, shuddered as if struck by a giant maul, and pitched onto his back. But already from Ki's lightning hand a dagger had soared, its blade striking ahead of the bullet. The robber had been hit, his neck skewered and jugular veins severed as he squeezed the trigger.

The robber crumpled, geysering blood. His amazed partner lurched forward and gaped at him, for a moment not comprehending what had happened. Jessie and Ki bored in then, and they spied the other figure hastily swing his revolver at them. They saw his muzzle flash, felt the wind of his passing lead. Jessie's Colt fired simultaneously, the two blasts blending as one. She missed by a hair, her target having jerked erratically aside at the last instant from nervousness and his pistol's recoil. The man reacted with a yelp and a stumbling twist, which saved him again as Ki's second dagger virtually scraped his ribs before sinking into the wooden wall behind him. Panicking, the robber whirled and disappeared in a frantic plunge down the path-way.

They sprinted to Nehalem, who lay flat and ominously still with a bloodied face and a bullet hole centered through his hatband. Crouching low, Jessie placed her ear against his chest.

"He shouldn't be," she said, "but he's still breathing."

21

"So is someone else who shouldn't be," Ki replied tersely, springing past the dead robber and into the mouth of the pathway.

Chapter 3

From the far end of the pathway came a blaze of gunfire.

Bullets whined by Ki as he slewed sideward against a wall, and Jessie sent two covering shots in return. Deafened by the reverberating fusillade, Ki hesitated for a moment and glanced back at the lane. Jessie was watching like a cat at a mousehole, her pistol held intently while she knelt alongside Nehalem who was beginning to stir feebly and make what Ki supposed were moanings and mutterings.

Tough old buzzard, Ki mused as he turned frontward, able to hear again. He listened, staring, but caught no sound or movement. Hugging the wall, he darted along the pathway and came to the far mouth without finding any sign of the second man, alive or dead.

At the corner he flattened and listened once more. This time he detected the pad of boots receding and not too far ahead. He charged forward, crossing another lane and diving into the next pathway. He was guided by the footfalls that were racing toward town. He continued this way, across lanes and through paths, spotting the kerchief mask but not the robber who'd discarded it while escaping.

Shortly the outskirts of dwellings tapered off, and Ki came out onto a bare field that served as rear yardage for the businesses fronting the main street. A dark figure was running behind the uneven row of buildings. Ki forged after him on noiseless feet, pursuing the man along a rutted wagon track from which the saloons and stores were serviced. He was gaining, but not enough to close the intervening distance before the man swerved and burst in through the back door of the Castle Dome. Ready for anything, Ki dashed toward the rear entry—then angled swiftly for some packing crates and ducked into a recess formed by their haphazard piling just as men emerged from the back door to stand on a stoop.

"I tell you, Willy's deader'n a poop," Ki overheard a voice breathless as if from running scared. "We stopped Nehalem and a coupla somebodies opened up and nailed us from the lane!"

"Who were they?" the other demanded in a raspy croak.

Peering cautiously, Ki glimpsed the companion of the one he'd killed and the paunchy torso and protuberant-eyed face of Frederick Tode. Well, that made sense; Froggy looted fools at gambling, according to Pollard, so why not loot lucky winners afterward?

Before the robber could stammer a response, Tode chewed into him again. "Were they passersby, Max? Were they strangers?"

"I, I dunno, boss. It was tar dark, and it all happened so fast. They were dressed reg'lar, like hands y'know, and one was kinda on the thin and short side. The other looked larger'n a barn door and is he gawdalmighty good with a knife. They can't finger me, honest. I had on my 'danna. I just didn't know what to do, boss, 'cept see you."

"Okay, come in and get with a coupla the boys for an alibi, just in case," Tode ordered, opening the back door. "Circulate like you don't know nothin', which'll be easy for you, and keep a distance from them two hombres if you spot 'em again." He ushered Max inside. The last words Ki heard were, "Tell me. I want a look at 'em."

Ki let them go. He was in poor position to attack and in no position to prove an attack justified by hard, legal evidence. Besides, another notion was beginning to percolate through his mind.

Speedily yet carefully, Ki retraced his steps and arrived without incident at the pathway to the livery stable lane. Collected about Jessie and Nehalem was a group that had been attracted by the shots. This first rush had attracted others behind whom more were converging, curiosity luring them from the street and saloons to stuff into the lane and add to the babble.

Ki elbowed his way through. Nehalem lay much as before, but now his hat was bunched as a cushion under his head, thereby exposing the blood-smeared gash that ripped his forehead and upper scalp.

"Just grazed him," Jessie said, still kneeling alongside.

"Just!" Nehalem growled and opened his eyes. He raised a trembling hand to his forehead, wincing as he gingerly traced the raw furrow. "Only just. If you hadn't thrown off that bandit's aim, his bullet would've dusted me plunk 'tween the eyes."

"My pleasure, believe me. How're you feeling?"

"Mite shaky. Jessie's fed me enough yarns to chipper me plenty, so reckon I'm willing to sit up if you're willing to help."

Ki slipped his arm under Nehalem's shoulders and lifted him to a sitting position. Plowing through the crowd loomed a bulky figure. Another moment and a barrel-chested man with gray-streaked hair and a salt-and-pepper handlebar mustache was frowning down at them, his sagging vest pinned with a silver badge marked Sheriff.

"Uriah, you look like a Commanche practiced scalpin' on you," the lawman declared gruffly. "The doc'll be here any minute now and tie up your noggin. Me, I best get to stumpin' after Latimer."

"You don't have to look far, Sheriff," a voice shouted nearby, and Glenn Latimer angrily shoved forward from the direction of the livery.

"Wouldn't done you no good trying to bolt far," the sheriff retorted. "I heard of your fracas at the Castle Dome, and that was bad 'nuff. But you can't get away with cold revengin' from ambush."

Before Latimer could argue, Nehalem cut in scathingly, "Must you always be stupid, Renwick? You're always jumping to conclusions. Fact is, I was held up. A coupla robbers took my cash and meant to kill me and would've if it weren't for Miz Starbuck and Ki here hornin' in. One skedaddled. The other's a stuck pig, lying near behind me."

"Dead and gone, eh?" The sheriff turned to Ki. "Gone where?"

"Down that pathway toward town." Ki hedged and was spared further questions by the bustling approach of Dr. Byron Augustas.

The crowd parted deferentially for him, and the energetic, little physician arrived with nary a ruffle to his elegant clothes — black frock coat, pearl-gray trousers and vest, and ruby stickpin thrust in his silk stock. Immediately he set to examining Nehalem, swabbing disinfectant to cleanse the wound of dried blood and bits of scalp.

Sheriff Renwick grimaced and traipsed off to investigate. Augustas worked deftly and soon had Nehalem on his feet, his head wrapped in gauze bandage. Repacking his satchel, the doctor prescribed in a sonorous voice: "Rest and change your dressing daily. If anything seems wrong, come see me, but I'm sure you'll be fine."

About then the sheriff returned. "Here's your roll, Uriah. Found it on the dead'un. Know him by sight as a saloon loafer, but not by name — yet. No chance of tracing his pard. He could've run out a dozen ways among these shacks or slipped into any one of 'em. Speaking of such, what were you doing around here, Latimer?"

"Saddlin' my nag at the livery and ridin' home."

"It's true," the hostler confirmed with a shout.

Jessie was nonetheless curious. Latimer never passed her in the lane, so he either took a peculiar back way there

26

or went long before for more than mere saddling—and neither alternative explained why, with the livery so near, he wasn't among the earliest to show up after the shots. Indeed, he came so late and back in the pack that he was lost from her view. However, Jessie decided not to question his story—yet.

And the sheriff was more contentious than suspicious. "My advice is to do precisely that and to stay out of town."

Latimer's eyes hardened. "Free country, Sheriff Renwick, where law is enforced fairly without favor or malice. Don't you forget that."

Sheriff Renwick blinked, shook his head. "I got enough upsets without lectures from contraries like you," he complained. Then he berated the crowd, "Okay, move, fun's done, clear out." Grumpily tugging at his mustache, he escorted the doctor along the lane to the street, herding the mob before him. "G'wan, move, I say!"

Both Latimer and Nehalem turned toward the livery, but Jessie was quicker this time to catch Latimer before he could disappear. He exchanged curt nods with Nehalem and then allowed Jessie to draw him aside, regarding her with cool, speculative interest.

Nehalem trudged on to claim his horse. Ki accompanied him until he put a stop to it. "Whoa up, dagnabit. I don't need a travelin' nurse. Besides, I'm already in your debt twice now." He eyed Ki shrewdly. "I believed you'd truly fallen over that spittoon, but I'm starting to reckon you don't fall down on much of anything."

"Spittoons can be pretty slick," Ki remarked dryly.

"Uh-huh. That's how I figure it—pretty slick." Nehalem chuckled as they shook hands. "Hope to see you soon. Drop by. You know my spread, of course, and I'd be open to negotiatin' a certain property with Miz Starbuck. Much obliged again, for everything."

Ki waited while Nehalem navigated the rest of the lane to the livery. Then Ki walked back to where Jessie and

Latimer were talking. Her lips were quirked; his were tight, his tone and manner civil as if determined to be polite about the axe that surely was to fall.

"You must be Ki," Latimer greeted him and then returned to finish addressing Jessie. "Come visit anytime. Why not, it's all yours."

Her eyes danced. "No, only a room is all, if one's to spare."

"There's Pa's old one; it's tidy. If you're in a mind to, you can ride with me tonight and cut some delay. I imagine you've got more important matters to dispose of." He paused significantly.

Ki said, "I think I'll stick in town and meet you at the ranch tomorrow morning. There're a few things I'd like to do here."

He did not offer to explain what they were. And Jessie wisely did not ask.

Chapter 4

After retrieving his traveling valise at the livery, Ki returned to the Castle Dome, got his key, and went upstairs to his room.

It was a simple, utilitarian room. It had the standard bed on which he dumped his valise, a mirrored bureau with a pitcher, basin, and an oil lamp which he lit, and a single, side window whose drapes he pulled closed. Then taking soap and a towel, he left for a quick bath down the hall and came back refreshed.

He was standing naked, pawing through his valise for fresh clothes, when he heard someone stop outside and tap softly on his door.

"Mr. Ki? Room service, Mr. Ki."

It was a girl's voice, pleasant and innocuous enough. But Ki had been lured before by sweet-sounding traps, and instinctively he checked that the drapes and lock remained closed and undisturbed, while padding to the door and clasping the towel modestly about his waist.

Still suspicious, he said, "I didn't order anything."

"Compliments of the management."

Cautiously he pressed his ear against the door panel. He heard no creak of shuffling boots and no low breathing of men lurking out in the hall with her and waiting to pounce. The girl said somewhat testily, "You going to let me deliver or make me keep yakking to myself?" Ki relented, warily unlatched, and then opened the door.

A young woman of twenty-two, maybe twenty-three,

slipped in. She leaned against the door, shutting it and re-locking it with her hands behind her. She smiled at Ki as she stepped toward him. She was not technically beautiful, perhaps—her black hair was a bit frizzled and her face was acne-pitted. But her black eyes were alert, her lips full, and her figure stretched the burgundy wrapper she wore, re-vealing intriguing curves and points of interest. She also looked vaguely familiar, and it took Ki a moment to place her as one of the girls he'd glimpsed working in the gentle-men's club downstairs.

She was not carrying anything. In fact, she appeared not to have come with anything period, save her wrapper and mule slippers. Ki said guardedly, "I'm not fit for visitors. What's the gag?"

"Oh, Verna's seen men in all states of undress," she replied, apparently referring to herself. "And it's no gag. The manager owes you one." She moved closer, letting her gown sweep back behind her. "On the house, the manager told me to tell you. A trick for a trick."

Ki couldn't help but smile. Verna was a sensuous prod-uct, provocatively packaged. She looked up into his face and he could see that she seemed not only willing, but eagerly anticipating her room service. She exuded sex, a blatant desire for it, and Ki reacted lustily.

"Some girls enjoy being undressed," she murmured coyly, now easing open the belt of her wrapper. "I'm not one of those. I want the touch, the feel. I want my fingers to strip off the layers until there's nothing more to hide, my flesh left naked and exposed."

The wrapper was unbuttoned. She shrugged it off her shoulders and let it slide slowly to her feet, revealing her smooth, round breasts and the crescent between her taper-ing thighs. She raised her arms slightly to hold his shoulder with one hand and loosen his grip on the towel with the other. The towel almost hooked upon his growing erection, which she regarded delightedly.

30

"Oh, you're fit. Lordy, are you fit."

She took his hand as she kicked off her mules, and led him toward the bed with all the practiced grace and speed of a professional hooker. Ki, wondering if he could break through that prostitute shell and stir the unloved woman beneath, swept in and smoothly lifted Verna into his arms. Initially she stiffened, afraid, and pushed against his chest. Then she relaxed as if she realized he was not some whooping bruiser who would hurl her down and leap on top of her. After removing his valise, Ki gently lowered her to the bedspread, sliding his hand free from her back and then moving it up along her arm and squeezing a nerve, which gave her a slight tingling sensation just before he let go of her wrist.

Ki enjoyed her reaction, the mixture of the tingle and his tenderness causing her to gasp, pleasured yet confused for a second. Joining her, he kissed her closed eyes while his hands cupped her breasts. His lips moved down the tip of her nose; his hands slid from kneading her nipples to stroke the cleft of her mound. She shuddered, arching, her own hand searching to rub his burgeoning shaft. She parted her mouth in readiness for his kiss. When he didn't kiss her as expected, she was taken aback, her professionalism faltering, her eyes questioning.

Then Ki kissed her with a warm, strong pressure. She seemed to resist his kiss as she had his carrying her—only to surrender quiveringly her emotions in greedy response to it. Whimpering, she wrapped her left arm around his neck, drawing him up and over her, the hand clasping his hardness guiding it into her crevice.

Ki felt himself sinking inside her a long way before he realized how tight she was. He paused and looked down at her. She was smiling blissfully from ear to ear. "Don't stop," she sighed, arching eagerly. "Lordy, this ain't the time to stop."

He lanced deeper into her again. He began to thrust very

31

hard and she seemed to grow tighter around him, until every time he would pound into her, she would moan and shiver from the squeezing impact. Yet she kept on smiling and undulating her buttocks, yearning for more. There was nothing indifferent or feigned about this union, Ki thought dizzily.

Verna's hips writhed and pumped under him, her thighs clenching him as if she would hold him in her forever. She began to pant and her eyes closed again, her fingers stroking his buttocks as she attempted to match Ki's quickening movements. Her breathless groans grew deeper, more prolonged, and she splayed her legs wider, bending her knees and locking her ankles above his back, rhythmically pummeling her heels against him to spur on his efforts. Then, as her guttural cries became continuous and throaty, her face contorted and her whole body trembled in a series of convulsions.

"Ahhh..." she mewed, as she compressed Ki's rampantly surging manhood, the force of her orgasm drawing the breath from her lungs. Ki burrowed deeper as he felt the girl's viselike grip spasming around him. With a final deep thrust, his own climax erupted far up inside her.

Slowly he settled over her soft warm body, crushing her breasts and belly while he lay, letting his immediate satiation wane. At last he rolled away, withdrawing from her, and he affectionately caressed her aching breasts. Verna smiled at him with languid, satisfied eyes.

"I thought I was fireproof," she whispered. "I was wrong." Shifting, she took his organ and began to study its flaccid length. "Hmmm. I see a good woman and a good man in your future."

Ki grinned. "What're you doing, fortunetelling?"

"Uh-huh. Like tea-leaf reading after the cup's drank, only more personal. More scientific. Every gent's is different, and each is a truer life line than is on a palm," she explained, continuing to consult his member. "The bad

32

man I see now is small yet dangerous, a rabid weasel. And I see a bad woman now, too." Arising then, she quickly slipped on her wrapper and mules. "That's all." At the door, however, Verna paused and gave a smile. "Except that the bad woman is a friend. G'night." She shut the door gently.

Ki looked at the door, then at himself, and broke up laughing. He still was chuckling moments later, after he had used pitcher water for a fast wash, dressed in clean clothes, and left his room.

He sobered when he reached the saloon. Glimpsing Tode at a rear poker table, he mulled over how to nail the high-play gambler, his earlier notion not having jelled into a solid plan yet, but staying stubbornly half-formed in his mind. He decided instead to keep close watch for a while, hoping Tode would try a similar robbery again.

It proved to be a tiresome and futile wait. Occasionally players came or went, but nobody appeared to win consistently at Tode's or any other game. Certainly no lucky sport left with sufficient spoils to trigger a heist by Tode's thugs. A few who looked owlhootish sifted through the crowd as though marking time for something to happen, yet Ki couldn't be sure they were in cahoots with Tode, for they didn't go near him, nor did the henchman Max show up and get friendly with them.

As the night progressed, the patrons grew fewer in number but tougher in type. Drunken, often heavily armed bravos guzzled glass after glass, their voices rising raucous and boastful as they made life increasingly difficult, and lucrative, for the bartenders and percentage girls—including Verna, Ki noted, who'd returned to duty. Fairly soon it would get so late or rowdy or both that the saloon would shutter, and Ki realized he could no longer afford to play his cards as given. He would have to deal his own hand if he wanted to rake in the fat pot called Froggy Tode.

So Ki wandered over and watched while Tode, two

husky laborers, a ranch hand, and a wispy-bearded youth finished their round of stud. At about the time one of the laborers folded, Ki had fashioned a scheme from his elusive notion. When the other laborer won, the youth got up, conceding he'd been wiped clean, and Ki sat down in his place.

"No oddball games, no wild cards," Tode said, shuffling the deck since it was his turn. "Raises limited to three of twenty each."

The ranch hand next to Ki added, "Let's see some stakes."

Ki laid down a sheaf of bank notes. "What's dealer's choice?"

Dealer's choice was ordinary draw poker, which was won by the same laborer. The deck passed to him, then the ranch hand, Ki, and on around, nothing much occurring for a short while. Ki looked for signs of cheating, but the game appeared honest with no ringers or marked cards. The play was desultory, the pots generally low and going back and forth, although the ranch hand was stewed and mostly lost, and Tode was sharp and won on average.

Ki was about to change the play when Max appeared.

Nobody at the table noticed the robber until Max came alongside Tode and stooped to whisper in his ear. Max tried to keep his face averted from Ki, but his sneaky sidelong glances made it obvious that he'd recognized Ki when he'd entered the saloon. His report earned a gruff, "Okay, now scram," and Max hurried away, while Tode regarded Ki with a fresh, covertly guarded interest.

From then on, the game was anything but so-so. The idea Ki had was to alter the play just enough so that the ranch hand would win bigger pots more often, until he became an unsuspecting victim for robbery. Ki did what he could to shift the odds accordingly. To his surprise, though, the ranch hand didn't seem to need his help, suddenly becoming blessed with phenomenal luck. And Tode, despite his skill, began to lose and kept on losing to everyone, especially the ranch hand. It was as though Max's brief presence had jinxed the gambler. The deal rotated around the table, but that didn't stop Tode's bad luck, nor did the game the dealer chose, nor the fresh decks Tode demanded.

The ranch hand lapped his winnings up, along with an unending flow of whiskey. His bad fortune became an increasing strain on Tode, and as time wore on, Tode began to growl out of the side of his mouth and to cheat whenever it was his turn with the deck. Once Ki determined a pattern to Tode's tricks, he was able to factor this against Tode and for the ranch hand. And the ranch hand's hot streak continued. When he'd stupidly fold a fantastic hand, the others would fold, too. When he'd stay and draw to an inside straight, he'd make them. And Tode lost constantly and with each hand grew angrier, almost to the point of confrontation.

Finally the ranch hand wavered upright. "Thash it, boys."

Tode leaned forward, flushed and furious. "Quitting, heh?" he snarled. "Prinzoni, no one can have your damnable luck."

The ranch hand hesitated, blinking uncertainly. Ki came to his defense, eyes cold and smile colder. "You calling it otherwise?"

The other players tensed, locked in their chairs. Tode gripped the table's edge with his fingers, an accusation hanging on his lips, but he didn't utter it. Instead, he stood rigid with frustration and glowering while Prinzoni shoveled his winnings into his hat. Ki also rose and started pocketing his remaining money.

"Hell, this game's busted," Tode said as Ki and Prinzoni turned to go. "It near busted me, too. I guess tonight's not my night." With a last malevolent scowl, he clomped toward a doorway, which, Ki surmised, led to some back quarters and the rear exit.

Ki headed for the front door, seeing Prinzoni weave to the bar. Max and five other bruisers trotted after Tode. Swiftly Ki went outside and to the building's corner and was about to dip down the narrow side alley when he heard Tode's croaky voice and the thud of boots approaching from the back. With careful haste, then, Ki retreated a pace and started shinnying up the corner support post of the boardwalk gallery, gripping the eaves and pulling himself onto the gallery roof, where he crouched out of view.

He was none too soon. Already Tode and his gunmen were hastening up the alley, and Tode was growling, "Want to get that slant-eyed knifer as much as I do Prinzoni. I'd swear he cheated, if I didn't know I was. Bemis, you and Max with me. The rest search uptown."

The two teams of three each split at the alley mouth, hunting along the main street for Ki or the ranch hand. Ki remained where he was, and sure enough, the gang soon regrouped below.

A gunman complained, "They must've flown the coop, boss."

"Maybe they never left the saloon," another suggested.

"Y'mean, nobody checked?" Tode snapped. "One of you go—"

Abruptly his mouth shut and he waved his men deeper into the alley shadows as a knot of patrons emerged from the saloon. They were yowling, "For he's a jolly good feller!" It was a rousing sendoff for the drunken Prinzoni, who kept grinning and stumbling.

"S'long, chums, s'long!" Prinzoni clapped on his cash-loaded hat and almost fell to his knees. "Gotta find m'hawse and ride!"

His barroom buddies went inside again to gargle their parched voices. The ranch hand staggered by the alley and on along the street, blearily eyeing the hitched horses and muttering to himself. "Lezzee, I rec'lect parking m'cayuse afront the El Mirage, I think."

Tode gave an ugly laugh. "C'mon, I'll show you how to handle this. Max and Willy bungled once tonight, but watch yours truly." He faded at a run back down the alley, followed by his henchmen.

Elbow was quieting, but some folks were still out and carousing about. Ki, peering over the edge of the roof, had to wait until nobody seemed to be noticing; then he swung around, dangled for a moment, and dropped lightly to the ground. Immediately he dashed after Tode and crew, who had turned at the far end of the alley and were moving in back of buildings on a course parallel to Prinzoni's. Ducking from nook to cranny, Ki slithered silently in pursuit.

Shortly Tode gestured and they veered between two darkened buildings. Ki approached gingerly, glimpsed them diving through the gloom toward the main street, then flitted past, and trailed them up the next alley. Arriving, he flattened against the corner, only a three-building span from where the gang now lurked.

The middle building of the three housed the El Mirage, a cantina looking pretty much done with trade for the night, though strumming guitar strings filtered plaintively through its closed door. Ki was watching when Prinzoni located his horse among the other mounts lined by the cantina, the ranch hand tripping in the gutter as he fumbled to untie the reins. Once they dropped loose, Ki saw Tode hurry out from his murky recess, duck under the rail, and move in on his prey. Max accompanied him, perhaps to redeem himself or for upclose training; the rest bunched on the boardwalk to watch and guard.

Ki glided forward in a shadow. Tode had caught his victim just as he was picking up his reins, and the bulk of the horses shielded them from view—and equally hid Ki's approach.

"Reach, cowpoke, and fetch off your hat!" Tode ordered. He now had a full-length duster buttoned over his identifiable gambler's garb and a kerchief across his even more recognizable face. He was backed by Max, who was also masked and armed. "Fast, damn it!"

"W—why, you shinewiders!" Prinzoni blurted tongue-twisted, but his hands flew to grasp his brim and wrench free his Stetson.

With Tode and Max concentrating on Prinzoni's tugging at his hat, it was Ki's moment to sweep in and strike. He launched between Prinzoni's horse and a skittish bay, his left hand gripping Tode in a hold that made him drop his revolver. The callused heel of his right hand smashed Tode in the bridge between his eyes. As Tode collapsed unconscious, Max whirled, cursing and centering his pistol. But already Ki was kicking out, his right foot slamming Max square in the balls. Shrieking, Max lurched backward, hunching and cupping his groin, blundering against the startled bay, and then crumpling under its stomping hooves.

Momentarily surprised but speedily recovering with angry alarm, the five on the boardwalk whipped revolvers and charged. Swiveling, Ki purposely knocked the muddled ranch hand off his feet and out of harm's way as slugs from the gunmen seared overhead. Yet they could not fire downward without hitting Tode, above whom Ki poised, a *shuriken* in hand. He snapped it toward the first gunman in sight, springing as he did so to the rail, then leaping at the next closest man, and catching him in the solar plexus with a flying kick. Clutching his hemorrhaging belly, the man fell to his knees, mimicking the first man, who'd toppled crouching as though in prayer, the *shuriken* protruding from his blood-spurting larynx.

"It's a trap—run for it!" a surviving gunman yelled, his cry drowned by the bellow of another: "Hell, I will! Take this!"

This was the telltale click of a hammer. And Ki, glimpsing the wink of cantina lamplight on steel as the defiant gunman cocked to fire, knew that while he pivoted he was too open, too late, to avoid the shot. Suddenly, grunting and scuffling, the boozy form of Prinzoni reared at the rail, Tode's discarded revolver wobbling in his fist as he blasted away. His incredible luck held, for it surely wasn't his skill or aim that sent a bullet drilling through the gunman's chest before the gunman could finish triggering.

After pausing only a second to breathe deeply in relief, Ki lunged at the fifth gunman, ramming his palm in a blow to the temple, fracturing the man's skull like an egg, and spearing shards of bone into his brain. The man died, standing. The last gunman, the one who'd bawled to run for it, was heeding his own advice by racing for the alley. Prinzoni emptied Tode's revolver more or less in that general direction. The gunman vanished, unscathed.

By now, shocked outcries were arising in response to the thunder echoing along the street. The few customers of the cantina were huddling agape in its doorway and against its dirty window glass. Ki ignored them, and after a swift scan assured him the four men on the boardwalk were cemetery fodder, he vaulted the rail and was gratified to find Tode was still breathing—raggedly, perhaps, with eyes scrunched and features waxen, but Tode would live. He had a lot to answer for, and Ki wanted to hear those answers.

Prinzoni wedged in beside Ki, swearing and stooping to look at Tode. "Y'know, Froggy's one helluva damn sore loser."

"Quick, tie his hands before he comes to," Ki said low and urgent, rolling the comatose gambler onto his stomach.

Rapidly sobered by the close squeak he'd had, Prinzoni stuck the revolver in his belt and tore off Tode's kerchief, using it to bind Tode's wrists securely behind him. Ki, meanwhile, glanced at Max's pulpy body under the bay. Then he warily gazed about in case the escaped gunman returned with allies to free their boss.

A few men already were grouping at the scene, but

these were from the cantina. More were rushing in along the street, but even at a distance, Ki could discern these were townsfolk, including the sheriff. Out of Quentin Pollard's office came the stout attorney and a smaller figure, Pollard turning toward Ki and the other man heading away in a spirited gait strongly reminiscent of Dr. Augustas' stride. No gunmen, however. Ki relaxed a little, any attempt to rescue Tode now impossible as people converged, collecting into a crowd.

Sheriff Renwick arrived and ogled the corpse-strewn boardwalk. "A massacre! Say, no, they've all got masks on. Another holdup!"

"Almost," Prinzoni corrected, grinning. "One vamoosed, but we downed those, and nabbed their honcho here—Froggy Tode."

His announcement caused a buzzing sensation. The sheriff let out a low whistle as he leaned peering over the rail. "It's Tode, okay." Then glimpsing Ki, he blurted, "You, again! You do this?"

"Well . . ." Ki turned and stared streetward at what he thought was a shiny purple phaeton being drawn out of town by matched chickasaws—the sort of ritzy carriage and team a celebrated physician might flaunt, but it was too far and too dark for more than a fleeting impression. "Maybe I helped a bit," he said. "Look, Tode's banged up and conked solid. Do you think we should get the doctor?"

"Alas, he left hours ago," Pollard interjected, coughing hoarsely and reaching for his tonic. "He's at his sanatorium."

"Let Tode suffer. Hanging's too good for him," Prinzoni declared and launched into an excited explanation of the events, ending as he began in a vociferous denunciation of the accused.

"I dast believe it." The sheriff sighed, reviewed the carnage, and then regarded Ki sarcastically. "You just happened by here, too?"

Ki shook his head and put on his amiable chump expression. "Happened to see Tode and his bunch following Prinzoni. Something about their attitude and the guns they wore drew my interest, I guess, on account of what happened before making me think such things. So I wondered if they were up to no good and tagged after. When they jumped Prinzoni, I jumped in." He finished off in a shrug.

"More'n jumped in, Ki. We nailed Tode to the fence, and it's plain he's a vicious bandit chief who is behind all the robbings and killings."

"Now, don't be too hasty," Pollard cautioned. "Perhaps Mr. Tode ain't no notorious crook, but was just tipsy and in a playful mood. After all, he didn't get away with your money, did he?"

"What!" Prinzoni was amazed. "Is that how you'll print it?"

"I tell you, I'd be afraid. Afraid of being slaughtered in my sleep by Tode's cronies. Such dangerous types are likely to go after anyone who attacks 'em and're liable to backshoot without warning."

"I ain't scared of Tode or nobody. I'll stand to testify, and I betcha Ki here ain't scared of telling the truth, either."

"Glad to hear your spunk," the sheriff told Prinzoni. "As for you, Pollard, Tode won't wriggle out of the charges. He'll draw ten to fifteen years for armed robbery, not some fine for disorderly conduct. You may fudge your story, but the word will spread, and I reckon most citizens'll think poorly of your newspaper then."

"The *Rainbow Register* is objective, neither flinching from the guilty nor flaying the innocent. The next issue will report you're convinced Tode can be held and convicted of felonious crimes, and I'd best be getting it into type." Pollard swigged his tonic, belched, and remarked, "Catarrh's bad tonight," while he waved a pudgy hand in a general adios and trudged on back to his office.

41

"No flinch or flay, eh." The sheriff gave a snort. "Hogwash. He was laying a defense and ragging a witness, if I'm not heap mistook. He knows Tode will want a good lawyer and'll hire him. His medicine's hogwash, too. Doctored corn squeezings. But it's no business of mine how'n where he buys his toots, so long as him and Doc Augustas behave themselves. Still'n all, I can't help pondering . . ."

"What?" Ki prodded.

"Oh, why a remote burg like Elbow gets so roisterous of a sudden, with thievings, killings, and Froggy Tode, and a sawbones, who's uppity enough to wipe a king's arse, pitching stench-water, magic dirt, and high-proof potions. Well, switch me, it's raining."

It barely was, the long-threatened storm beginning as a light sprinkle. Sheriff Renwick, assisted by willing hands, quickly picked up Froggy Tode, and they carried the senseless gambler to the jail.

Ki, trailing along to make sure there was no mistake, watched as the sheriff opened a little cell and threw Tode into the tiny cubicle. "Now we'll soon find out who're Tode's cronies," he mused as he left the law office. By now the rain had become a slow, soaking drizzle that seeped through his clothes and left his skin damp. Weak flashes of lightning played over the heavens, white talons stabbing down toward the western expanse of the valley. Ki enjoyed the crackling display above the dark, sleeping town while he walked back to the Castle Dome.

Customers were still drinking at the bar, but nobody was at the gaming tables. Tired girls sat around, waiting for quitting time, while bartenders cleaned up the mess after the night's fun. Verna wandered over and settled in the chair across from Ki.

"My feet," she groaned, rubbing them and then leaning her chin on her hand and eyeing Ki with weary coyness. "I sorely do need to rest 'em. Would you be interested in

42

treating this bad woman like a friend and taking her some-where comfy so she's off her feet? I mean, that is, if you're feeling fit and up for it."

Ki was up for it.

Chapter 5

Much earlier that evening, Latimer said, "We're coming to the Box L now."

Astride her roan, Jessie shifted, leaning as she concentrated on the view ahead. The night was slightly overcast so that little moonlight or starshine filtered through the veil of cloud. Yet stretching westward from the trail, until they vanished over a rise, were stout strands of rusty barbed wire stapled firmly to well-planted posts. The wire right-angled directly ahead and paralleled the trail into the distance. Beyond the wire, she perceived numerous low ridges breaking through the valley plateau. Their slopes were littered with boulders; their earthen banks and the surrounding depressions were thatched with short grasses, brush thickets, and scrub trees, and were dotted with plump sheep.

"Your flock looks in top shape," Jessie observed.

"It is. Pa taught us how to tend sheep right. These aren't quite as prime as our main herd in Weed Canyon, which ain't a far jog off our path. I have no need to ride that way, but I have no need not to."

Jessie laughed. "My favorite reason for going somewhere."

"Okay, we will." He lapsed quiet for a moment and then chuckled nostalgically. "Yeah, Pa hated sheep bad as any puncher till he learned they made money by fattening on land that'd starve a cow, so he figured raising 'em and marrying beat cowdogging alone and poor. He started in

New Mexico, where me 'n Dwight were born, but wanted to move after Ma passed away. Pa sure knew what he was doing, buying this piece. He was turning profit here right up to his death."

"Excuse me if I'm prying too personal, but I've heard your father grew sick and heard he got shot. How did he die?"

Latimer hesitated, looking a trifle uncomfortable. "Some of both, I reckon. First, he was shot. Somebody cut our wire and let the sheep onto Nehalem's range. Caused a bit of a ruckus, but no one hurt, Pa's orders being not to shoot for keeps unless forced to. Anyhow, he was bushwhacked the next dawn. We thought he'd recover, but he just kept on lingering, worsening, till he gave up the ghost."

"I'm sorry." Jessie nodded gravely. "I understand."

"Not fully, Miss Starbuck."

"Jessie, please."

"Miss Starbuck," he repeated firmly. "Pa died of a fight we aren't fighting. We got no feud, no attack going against anybody. But he got shot and is the only one who did so out of a dozen such sniperings at us. Wires keep getting cut. Sheep are butchered and poisoned by saltpeter, which is harmless to cattle, y'know. If those cow wranglers would only leave us in peace, we'd do fine, but they won't, and now you've come to finish off what they can't. So excuse me for being personal, but I ain't exactly thrilled at seeing you here 'n now."

Jessie smiled good-naturedly, not humorously. "Maybe you'll be glad you did see me before the last sheep is shorn."

Latimer flexed his shoulders. "I doubt it," he growled, and spurred his chestnut stallion ahead in a nimble trot.

Jessie kicked her roan forward to stay apace, taking no offense at Latimer's gruff abuse. His reproach, in fact, confirmed her initial impression of him as an honest man

45

deeply attached to his land—to his roots, as he'd called them, which kept him anchored to the basic values of his life. He stood tall; he didn't slink. He was smart; he wasn't sharp. And his rejection of her perversely attracted her, challenging her to win his approval, arousing a closer awareness of him that bordered on sexual interest. Not that she had any such intentions in mind, she thought hastily; her mission was strictly business and that's how it'd be, uncomplicated.

The cloud veil gradually thickened, becoming a sooty blanket hooding the sky by the time Latimer led Jessie into Weed Canyon.

As they passed through its narrow entrance, he dropped back to ride alongside her. Calmly, as if he'd never lost his temper, he explained the ranch's name for the canyon derived from its abundance of weeds. Sheep ripened on them, including the larkspur, which was deadly to cattle, and the canyon could accommodate any size herd the Box L could muster. Its lower end drew together in a bottleneck and was heavily fenced with barbed wire. Otherwise, there seemed to Jessie to be thousands of contented woolies grouped where the canyon widened out into a broad, elongated, natural grazing pen.

The blackening clouds continued to roll lower, and it began to sprinkle gently like a breezy mist. Jessie and Latimer closed in on a large campfire, around which four herders lounged, smoking and talking. The men cast questioning glances at Jessie, but when Latimer introduced her, their uncordial responses made it plain they were aware of who she was. In turn, Jessie smiled infectiously as she met lanky Jackson Roget, carrot-haired Brick Noone, Big Fletcher, who was huge, and finally Glenn Latimer's brother. Dwight Latimer was a strapping young man in his early twenties, his features like his brother's, though his eyes were more sullen.

"I'll dish us some chuck," Glenn Latimer told her. "We

can set here awhile, and let you get some feel for routine."

Jessie laughed, but didn't try arguing him out of his wrong notion about her. From the pot, he filled two twin bowls with a thick stew of mutton, which he served with biscuits.

Nobody minded the sprinkle until it developed into a drizzle. Lacking tents or slickers, they cloaked themselves in blankets and proceeded to ignore the rain. First, however, the crewmen made sure their pistols and carbines were protected. They were ex-cowhands drawn by the Box L's higher wages and took vigilant effort to earn their fightin' pay. And just as they'd overcome their aversion to sheep, they started to overcome their aversion to Jessie, who sat and ate uncomplaining—while Glenn Latimer acted as if he feared she might melt and Dwight brooded as if he hoped she would.

The breeze died to a wet, sultry hush. But now thunderclouds were encroaching over a skyline that increasingly flashed with streaks of heat lightning. There came the distant rumble of thunder that warned them of a summer electrical storm. The herd sensed it and grew restless but not spooked, sheep being either smarter or dumber, depending on one's outlook, than more panicky cattle.

Jessie finished her stew as the shower swelled to a downpour. Latimer suggested they head out before it got worse, and Jessie was about to agree when Big Fletcher suddenly stood up, cocking his ear.

"I heard sumpin'," he said. "You hear anythin'?"

They all listened with him.

"Some moving back in the canyon," Brick agreed momentarily. "Sounds almost like gallopin' horses, but that can't be right."

The noise out of the night grew louder, more distinct. Big Fletcher bellowed, "Them's are horses! Up'n at 'em, you duffers! We got scalawags bustin' down 'pon us under cover of the storm!"

Everybody scrambled to his feet, clutching for weapons as the raiders bore in from the darkness. Rifle fire began blazing and the sheep began bleating, and the herders sprang for their horses staked nearby. "Hold 'em off while I git the lady outta here!" Glenn Latimer ordered, grabbing Jessie by the hand. But she slipped free and dived for her roan, leaving Latimer yelling and cursing, unable to do other than follow her lead and mount up.

The six counterattacked, cutting loose with their carbines. This merely added to the pandemonium. The horses of friend and foe alike tore through the frightened confusion of bedded sheep, sending most scattering, injuring others, and trampling some to death.

And as if this were not enough, chain lightning sundered the sky above the canyon. It struck the middle of the herd and the thunder crashed with it, and in that same second, every last sheep was up afoot and running. The ground trembled as if jarred by the gigantic fist of an earthquake. The darkness was ripped by blinding light. The rain descended in a solid sheet. Hell broke apart there in the canyon, and the stampede was on.

Shaken by the lightning and struggling with balky horses, the six were surprised by the bolting herd. They were suddenly trapped in a surging morass of sheep, facing one bunched swarm looming directly at them. They wrenched their mounts in a swerving dash to avoid the onrushing flock, their reaction too swift for talk. None was needed. Jessie had experienced cattle charges before and felt the same tension and dread now as then. It didn't matter that cows bulked over sheep; sheep still bulked over humans. May God help the riders caught in their path—or worse, in their midst, as she and the others were, for though that one tight group missed them and brushed on by, more sheep rushed perilously close in an increasing tide. It was almost more than she or any of them could do to maneuver their plunging horses out of the way.

Lightning again struck, turning black to white. By its dazzling incandescence, they saw a compact body of riflemen just pulling to a halt some distance ahead. Weapons blasted on both sides. Jackson Roget reeled in his saddle, clipped by a bullet. One of the raiders pitched sideward from his horse to lie like a sack of old clothes. His partners wheeled and retreated, shooting.

The defenders spurred after—Box L horses bucking and shying; Jessie's roan dancing, ears laid back and eyes wild. Frenzied sheep veered around and between, a blundering throng of clacking horns and slashing cloven hooves churning past them. Some lost their footing and fell beneath the kicking maul of other sheep. The bawl of the crippled mingled with the drum of hooves and the claps of thunder. Mud was underfoot and the rain was torrential, driven by wind gusts that swept the canyon with howling fury.

Drowned and deafened by the furor, the cracks of renewing rifle fire pierced through, muted and faint. Yet their message was loud: The raiders had backed, not fled, into the darkness. Jessie doubted they had forecast the storm and timed their attack to coincide, but they nonetheless were taking full advantage of it, threatening the Box L with a more lethal danger than nature was causing.

She glimpsed Dwight Latimer about a hundred feet away and read his set, blanched face in the glare of the lightning. He was game enough, but was shocked and bewildered by the whirlwind of his first stampede. The tumult of sheep breaking in front and beside him muddled his wits, and in confusion he kept trying to hold back his horse, while his horse kept fighting to thrust and run.

Jessie shouted to Glenn Latimer and pivoted her roan toward Dwight. Glenn swore at her, his brother, and then himself as he followed her angling plunge across the main flow of the herd.

Jessie reached Dwight just as his horse began to falter.

49

She shoved alongside to brace its stumble, yelling at Dwight to give his horse its head, but he was too rattled to understand. Leaning, Jessie tugged the split-ear headstall off the horse and yanked the bridle reins from Dwight's grip. By then Glenn had come. With a slap of the reins, they hazed Dwight and his horse straight on through the herd into the range of gunsights.

Dwight clung to the saddlehorn, his unleashed horse striding heedless of the slippery muck and routing sheep and straining Jessie and Glenn to keep pace. The Box L crewmen were dim blurs ahead and to one side. The raiders were invisible. Ferocious bursts of thunder numbed their ears, lightning and rain blinding their eyes.

Then abruptly Glenn stood in his stirrups and pointed with his carbine. A trio of riders was moving toward them at a hard trot, long guns in hand. A flare of lightning showed the features of a short, heavyset man, another with a black patch over one eye, and a third with a face full of untrimmed whiskers. Glenn twisted with a savage grin and yelled at Jessie, "Here comes our lobo meat!"

Jessie felt less confident, for by that same flash, she glimpsed a second bunch advancing on the yonder ranch crew. Before she could respond, however, the lightning-riven night shot a bolt so close that it stunned their senses. The horse carrying Dwight, crazed with fear, tore off, heading for the approaching riders. Swaying and jerking, Dwight groped desperately for the slack reins, although all his tugging on them couldn't check so mad a run. His only prayer was to hang on dearly until his horse played out or fell with him.

Immediately Jessie and Glenn chased after Dwight. They saw the raiders quicken and open fire, missing Dwight, for they were unable to aim effectively while jouncing asaddle. Yet Dwight and his berserk horse were on a collision course and inevitably would be hit within moments. They loosened answering salvos, hoping to dis-

50

tract if not to strike and aware that at a gallop from a greater distance they had less accuracy than the raiders. The whiskered man winged some slugs their way, but mostly the shots targeted Dwight. They heard the crewmen swapping lead with the other raiders, their rolling beat of gunfire a muffled blending with the storm. And Dwight and these raiders seemed farther, an eternity away.

Then Dwight's horse lurched, tilting, as if both left legs had gone from under it. They saw Dwight waver drunkenly in the saddle. The horse keeled over, throwing Dwight clear just before collapsing on its side, legs twitching. Dwight lay in a motionless, shapeless bulk in the mud.

The raiders tossed a couple of passing bullets at Dwight as they rode by. Then they turned their mounts toward Jessie and Glenn, charging with their rifles spewing smoke and flame.

Glenn Latimer responded by levering and triggering his old Winchester '73. Jessie felt the breech of her new '76 growing warm from punishment and wondered if it meant trouble or a trait, this being the first she'd used the carbine since buying it in Tucson. In any case, she thought, their Winchesters lacked the range of the bewhiskered gent's Sharps .50 rifle. His sidekicks appeared to be wielding Spencer .56-50 repeaters, which could deliver plenty of grief, but his Sharps could really reach out and punch.

The raider proved her point by reaching out and punching her horse in the chest. The roan took a final few paces dead on its feet, allowing Jessie to kick free of the stirrups and land on her knees in the mud. Then it plunged, folding frontward, and somersaulted.

Jessie dived behind the dead horse, and as the three raiders rode her down she lay flat until they came within Winchester range. Their bullets thumped into her dead horse, one puncturing the saddle cantle and buzzing her cheek. Then they were on top of her and she was shooting with swift desperation. Her first slug smashed the short

51

man in the face. She kept firing and the man's rifle flashed once into the air as he flopped backward from his saddle and, with a coughing death rattle, tumble to the ground.

Glenn was slewing and sheering his chestnut stallion in erratic fits and starts to confuse the raiders. It was working, Jessie saw, as she caught glimpses of his maneuvers; their shots were snapping and whining after him—before, above, and below him, everywhere but in him. Yet she knew his antics couldn't last forever, that like his brother, he was trapped by inexorable time.

Then Glenn stopped suddenly. Jessie almost missed it, the halt was so abrupt. And once more the raiders were thrown off, but this time Glenn had a stationary perch under him. He took aim with his carbine as the one-eyed man shifted, and he shot the man twice and then spurred toward the whiskered man, still firing. The man with the eyepatch slumped, and his horse drifted on.

The whiskered man lay low along his horse's neck. His Sharps lanced flame and a bullet perforated Glenn's hat. Glenn shot twice and his carbine clicked on an empty magazine. He dropped it and drew his Colt revolver, but he had problems and looked it.

Jessie knew it. At best, the range between the men was about a hundred yards and too far for a revolver. The whiskered man could simply retreat to five hundred yards or more and riddle Glenn.

The whiskered man had ridden past and was having trouble pulling up his horse. Jessie rested the barrel of her carbine along the side of her dead horse, aimed it at the man, and squeezed the trigger. She missed. She levered another cartridge into the breech and shot again. The man stiffened upright and reined his horse around and Jessie shot him again. This time her bullet hit a vital spot and the whiskered man let go of the reins and grabbed his belly with both hands. His horse lunged forward and he was pitched sideways, and Jessie thought she heard his neck crack when she saw him land.

Glenn rode over. He had retrieved his carbine and was reloading it with fumbling, muddy fingers. "Sorry about your horse."

"I'm not. Horses can be replaced. But dead men can't come back, period. All our sorrow is better reserved for your brother."

"Thanks, Jessie." He paused, the vague noise of the gunfight still raging yonder and piercing the storm. "I want to go see Dwight for a moment. Then I gotta hightail over and help my crew before there are more deaths to be sorry over. If you'd like to join me, why, I'd be pleased. Just grab a spare nag."

Glenn waited while Jessie snagged the short, stocky raider's mount, which happened to be the closest available. The saddle was molded to a different butt and the stirrups hung too low, but the horse was sturdy and easy-natured and got her where she pointed it.

Dwight Latimer lay as he'd landed, on his back with arms outstretched, eyes closed. There was no sign of the horse.

"Swipin' a horse carcass, don't that beat all," Glenn marveled as he dismounted. He crossed to stand over his brother in grim reflection. "Well, we got 'em, Dwight, a fat lot of good it does you."

"Curious," Jessie murmured. "I don't see any blood, any visible wound." Same as she had with Uriah Nehalem, she knelt and put her ear to Dwight's chest. "He's breathing."

"Of course, I'm breathing," Dwight whispered hoarsely, still not moving. "It's all I can do right now."

Glenn was flabbergasted. "Can't be! You're shot dead!"

"I got tossed on my noggin. Don't bother me."

"I'll bother you lots. Make me think you was a corpse,

53

will you. Now your horse is gone, and I know I saw it shot and go down."

"Naw, that treacherous gluefoot slipped and fell in the mud. If it ain't here, I 'magine it probably wandered off for shelter." It took him a few minutes, but Dwight slowly sat up. He coughed, threw up a small quantity of rain water, and then gingerly felt his left temple. It was a raw goose egg, pulpy from his impact.

"Are you sure you're okay?" Jessie asked.

"I reckon," Dwight replied, wincing. "A twister of a headache. Other'n that, nothing particular feels snapped or busted."

"What luck," Glenn said.

Luck. That unpredictable factor again, Jessie thought while they trudged in search of the horse. It was bad luck for Dwight to have ridden that horse and unbelievably good luck he hadn't been shot or truly injured. How do you gauge it? How do you figure it?

It took longer to catch the horse than it did to find it, but Dwight was determined to show it who was boss and won the first round by getting back aboard. They rode, then, to the herders who were beleaguered but still alive. Rain fell, a last deluge before it began tapering off as quickly as it had begun. Lightning speared, thunder erupted, then the blackness was back, and the thunder rumbled into silence.

They followed the gunfire. The three herders, they found, were holed up in one of the rare outcrops along the canyon floor, undoubtedly having made a fighting dash for it when first attacked out in the open. The outcrop was under seige by four raiders, a fifth sprawled lifeless off to one side, but what with the night, the storm, and the rock cover, it appeared to have become a stalemate.

Their approach changed all that. The raiders saw them coming, and for a brief, confused moment a brutal skirmish broke loose, long guns barking. The next moment, the raiders were ducking and weaving for their horses, snatching reins and leaping for leather and fleeing down the canyon.

They whipped after the raiders, but by the time they reached the outcrop, the raiders were merely flitting silhouettes, shooting and yelling in headlong retreat, a riderless horse pounding after. The herders clambered out from the rocks and joined them in speeding the raiders on their way with blistering fusillades. The click of beating irons faded swiftly in the distance. The six did not attempt pursuit, but with the aid of torches, busied themselves in taking stock of the damage already done.

The men had numerous scratches, contusions, sprains, and cuts, but the only serious injury was the flesh wound through Roget's left forearm. Brick Noone came though unscathed, though like the rest, his expression was bitter, his green eyes seething with resentment.

"Tonight Nehalem's gone too far," he growled. "He sent 'em here to burn powder, and he needs getting burned with some hisself."

The others chorused their support, suggesting vengeful plans. Jessie was not surprised; they had swallowed a great deal of punishment and had reached the limit of their endurance. She surveyed the Box L men with understanding and empathy before she spoke.

"Didn't it ever occur to any of you," she said quietly, "that this is precisely what sombody might want you to go do?"

Roget scoffed, "Nehalem mayn't want us, but he'll get us."

"And you are Box L crew. Were the raiders from Nehalem's crew? No cowhand I ever saw even fights as they did, but I don't know his men. You must. You've got four bodies to tell by, and if they're Nehalem's, we've a case for the law. If they're not, then whose men are they?"

Glenn shrugged resignedly. "Okay, lady, we'll go look."

The dead raider by the outcrop was studied first. He was

unknown to the men, which intrigued them enough to ride and examine the other three. These also were strangers with ordinary clothing and equipment and nothing significant in their pockets or gear.

"No personals, no items linking them to anyone," Jessie stated. "That's crooks' ways. They were hired solely to do dirty work."

Glenn muttered in puzzled exasperation. "Against us? The Box L isn't worth squat except for sheep, and Nehalem's the only person hankering after it. So if not him, Jessie, then who else? And why?"

"I don't know. We'll have to dig to find out. But if you act on the way things appear on the surface and go hit Nehalem as a payback for tonight, you'll trigger a feud that's apt to grow into a range war. I've a hunch that's what somebody is after. Glenn, please promise me that the Box L won't do anything rash."

"How can I? I don't own it; I don't have control."

"Maybe not officially, but you do have say. I'm asking that we all work together to clear up this mess before it blows up. If we don't and it does, some of us are likely to go with it."

Glenn eyed Jessie sharply and then scanned the men. "Y'know I swore I'd do nothing for Starbuck, but p'raps she's right. P'raps we best sit tight and see what's what. I'd hate to make a mistake. We can always rip the lid off later, but once it's ripped, we can't never put it back on." He paused while reluctant agreement was voiced, even Dwight nodding with grudging approval. Then he said, "Okay, that's settled. Now let's go gather in them fool sheep."

Chapter 6

Jessie sat in bed reading her book.

The bed was the personal four-poster of late Thaddeus Latimer and was for Jessie a blessed relief after a day that began riding to a funeral and ended by chasing sheep. The stampede proved costly, for many sheep were dead and many others were so badly injured they had to be shot. It proved exhausting as well, chousing sheep through rain and mud until most were milling and bleating back in their canyon bed.

Glenn tried convincing his brother to go home and call it a day. But Dwight was adamant; he was on nighthawk duty, and the devil with his bashed head. So Glenn and Jessie left by themselves, and after a slog south along a quagmired trail, they entered a grove of lofty cottonwoods. There, clustered about a well, were the wood-and-adobe Box L *casa* and its corresponding outbuildings.

The main house was sparsely furnished, though neat and scrubbed. The bedroom given Jessie was in keeping with the house, the four-poster, dresser, wardrobe, and commode being about it. The patchwork bedspread, the chintz window curtains, and the several stitched Bible quotations on the walls lent color to the otherwise plain room.

The parlor sidewall was comprised of a massive fireplace. They fetched wood, lit a blaze there, then filled kettles with water, and suspended them from the spit. As the water was heating, Glenn placed a heavy tin tub, soap, and towels near the hearth, while Jessie brought in her canvas bag that she'd retrieved from her dead roan before leaving the canyon.

When Jessie came out of the bedroom with her toiletry kit and nightgown in hand, Glenn was pouring steamy water into the tub, and he said, "Ain't the hugest bath. Ain't the peak of modesty, either."

Jessie smiled. "Why, Glenn, it's what we make of it."

"True, true." He put the kettles aside, a playful grin on his lips. "Or what we don't make of it. I'll go, uh, tend the horses."

After he went outside, closing the door behind him, Jessie shed her clothes in a pile on the floor and eased into the hot water. She washed carefully, thoroughly, every inch of her voluptuous body. After lathering her hair, she stepped out of the cramped tub and knelt beside it to rinse off. Then she briskly toweled dry and slid her nightgown over her head. It was a long, flowing style, but evidently its fine nainsook cloth had shrunk when last laundered, because now Jessie discovered that it fit as if a size too small. She smoothed it out as best she could, the fabric like a lover's clasp around her bosom and bottom.

She was gathering her clothes when Glenn knocked from outside. "I'm decent," she called, and the door opened in back of her. She heard him gasp. Belatedly realizing she was bent and that the taut fabric displayed her buttocks and legs, she hastily straightened, holding her bundle to her breasts as she turned. "Well, I thought I was decent," she said with teasing chagrin. "If I'm not, you be decent and don't peek."

Glenn nodded vaguely, a little glassy-eyed. Jessie padded barefoot to the bedroom, sensing a perverse response to the choking sounds Glenn was making behind her, an intriguing tingle worming up through her flesh. She was dead tired but all woman, and she relished the sensation of being attractive to the few men she found desirable. And heavens, Glenn Latimer was certainly desirable!

Her bedroom door shut, she discarded her clothes and stood in front of the wardrobe mirror, brushing and pinning up her damp hair so she could sleep on it. Then from her bag she took a book, climbed into bed, and began studying the book's pages, pausing now and then to concentrate on a particular entry.

Her book was a small back ledger which she carried whenever traveling and was a condensed copy of the larger original book kept at her Circle Star Ranch. Between the leather covers were the names and activities of a vicious international crime ring that was intent upon seizing control of America's commerce and politics. Her father had begun compiling the information while in the Orient, during his first meager years of building what would ultimately become the Starbuck business empire, and he had maintained the original book ever since. In his subsequent struggles with this cartel, his wife was killed while Jessie was a babe, and eventually, he, too, fell its victim. By then, however, Jessie was a young woman, mature enough to understand his persistent fight and resolute enough to carry it on afterward, aided by Ki and her inherited wealth —and helped by the book, which she scrupulously continued to update and revise from current investigative reports or through her personal experiences.

Nothing Jessie had learned previously from the notebook or reports indicated that either Latimer or Nehalem was involved with the cartel. She checked the entries for them again anyway and for mention of anyone else she'd met so far. She soon found a reference concerning Froggy Tode made by her father some seven or eight years before.

It was short but sweet: TODE, Frederick, age & origin unknown. Ruthless; fair leader; varied pursuits. Main occup. lone gambler. Occas. headed (heads?) gangs preying on Chisholm, Shawnee, Western trails for cartel rustling syndicate. Last scrape Dodge City for cheating and shilling. (Dr. Zack Terwilliger's Tapeworm Elixir). Sightings also in Wichita, Abilene, Newton.

The entry made her consider possibilities, contemplate connections, and start leafing through for cross-references. She hesitated once, brought up by the whoop of riders outside and the splash of Glenn in the tub. The noises passed, so she returned to reading, but she located nothing more of interest. She was still absorbed in her book, however, when minutes later a rapping sounded on her door.

"Are you," Glenn called hesitantly, "are you asleep?"

"Not yet. Come on in." Jessie stretched to put her book aside, trying to clasp the sheet modestly around her while watching Glenn enter and shut the door. He was clad only in clean pants; the muscular power of his naked torso gleamed in the lamplight.

"Hope I ain't disturbing you, Jessie, but I got disturbed by pondering. Like, how'd you know the raiders weren't Nehalem's crew?"

"I didn't know. I guessed that when you didn't seem to recognize them right away. Even if they'd been, they could've been working on their own, without Nehalem being aware, but I doubted it. They'd have known they'd be stuck in the middle if ever caught. Now I have a question. Who were those riders I heard outside a few minutes ago?"

"Oh, just Brick and Jackson. They'n me are the day crew—for a while, anyhow; we take turns pulling night'n day duty—but since not much goes on here, we gen'rally stick around and bull with the next shift. That's why they chanced to be in the canyon, thank God." Glenn chuckled low. "If they'd been raiders, I'd have shot in here to bodyguard. You're a brave lass, Jessie, 'cept a mite tetched."

"I guard my own body, thanks. Why am I crazy?"

"Well, mayhaps I'm being overly harsh. You done proved you can handle yourself, I grant. What I meant was, I can't fathom your logic for counting out Nehalem. So what if the raiders weren't his crew? He's got the money to hire 'em and the land to roost 'em."

"Nehalem's a salty old shorthorn, the sort who hits straight from the shoulder. I can see him rearing and charging to have it out with the Box L at any time, but to poison sheep and import gunswifts for sneak attacks, no." Jessie shifted to the far side of the bed and patted the empty space. "You look awfully uncomfortable, Glenn. Come here and sit down. There's plenty of room."

He didn't respond at once. "Your logic is sensible far as it goes, Jessie, but it don't stretch to explain who else it might be," he then said and began to pad closer. "Folks don't risk the hoosegow or hemp rope just to kick up a row for nothing. Certainly not for this place, and no matter what sort of ruckus they whumped up, they couldn't expect to chase Nehalem out."

"Maybe they don't particularly want us or Nehalem. Maybe they are simply using what's available." Jessie swallowed, the grace of his motion, the strong muscles flexing along his thighs and chest, the hardness of his loins sending soft chills up along her spine. She pressed on: "The bad blood between our spreads is well known, and cattle-sheep feuds are so common that ours would go unquestioned. Maybe we're a smoke screen to divert attention from something they do want badly. If we could figure out what that something is, we'd be a long way toward solving this mess."

"That's another thing, why are you bothering? I can't reckon it. You'll be closing down the Box L and getting rid of the sheep."

"Sheep are all right, if tended properly." She smiled as he sat gingerly at the edge of the bed. "There, now, more comfortable?"

He nodded. In one sense, he was very comfortable because the groin of his pants was blatantly tented out. Spying his arousal caused Jessie's nipples to harden involuntarily, and she thought dizzily: It must be something else! Hastily she glanced higher, only to see Glenn's eyes roaming the contours of her breasts.

Their gazes met, locked. A pause lengthened.

Glenn finally cleared his throat. "Er, funny you saying that about sheep. Cow ranchers usually don't like 'em. Maybe you ain't crazy, Jessie, but you sure are a funny cow rancher."

She said, "But Starbuck's into many operations besides cows." She smiled dreamily again and glanced idly about. "You think your father would mind me sleeping here?"

"Ah, no. Pa always liked ladies in his bed. Er, that is . . ."

He lapsed into lame silence, and another pause developed, each aware of the other and enormously stirred by nearness and feeling. And in that electric moment, Jessie knew she was no longer tired, that her blood was filled with a fire that flamed through her flesh and goaded her to reckless abandon.

"Glenn," she purred, "if you dare try to kiss me . . ."

He stiffened as if she'd read his mind. "Y—yes?"

"If you do, then I won't dare to try kissing you first."

There was an impact as their bodies crushed in an embrace, her arms curling around his neck, her tingling breasts pressing against his chest, her mouth insistent and bruising against his. He moaned slightly, deep in his throat, his hands gliding down her back to stroke the little cleft at the top of her tensing buttocks. Jessie found that she was moaning a little too.

His hands then gently and firmly began to lift up her nightgown. "You have too many clothes on," he murmured, bunching the gown higher, then over her head, and off her upraised arms. He stared at her breasts, exclaiming, "By gawd, you got dandy teats!" He cupped them, his fingers kneading gently. His head bent, his lips kissing and then sucking each distended nipple hungrily.

Jessie groaned, her head swaying back and forth. "You have too many clothes on, too," she gasped, her hands reaching for his pants, fumbling to undo the buttons of his fly. Tender and gentle, her fingers drew out his erection and began to stroke its fleshy shaft. Still rubbing him with one hand, she used her other to push his pants down, until reluctantly, he had to stop nursing on her breasts and finish taking his pants off. He threw them aside and crawled onto the bed, one wildly excited male.

Again his mouth engulfed each breast in turn, his tongue licking her nipples. Then he wandered lower, kissing her navel, trailing on till his lips were browsing on her loins, sliding back and forth, deeper, his tongue plunging into her.

Jessie shuddered, her breathing erratic, ragged. Her legs splayed wider, bending at the knees to give him fuller access. Her sensitive flesh felt Glenn press his mouth closer. He was greedy and nibbling. His tongue was everywhere. Jessie swooned. A minute . . . two minutes . . . her belly rippled. She began to pant explosively. Her loins curved up, pressed up with trembling tension to force that stroking tongue tighter to the vibrant center of her body.

And Jessie climaxed. She wailed and twisted in the grip of her sweet agony, her writhings never breaking with the tongue and lips that were consuming her in ecstasy. Then with a final stroke from bottom to top, Glenn lunged up over her, and her hands clutched at his hardness, guiding it eagerly to the entrance of her empassioned hollow.

His thick goad stabbed into her. Jessie twitched, feeling impaled, an agony of pleasure that grew sharper and tighter the deeper he skewered into her. She could feel his pulse from it. Glenn breathed through his mouth, hugging her, forcing his girth into her hot depths, her insides igniting as he buried all of his huge invader.

His strong movements began at once. Straining and pistoning, his buttocks flexing, he hammered into her in a savage lust that rocked them both with squirming convulsions. Jessie spread her thighs and pulled her knees back to her shoulder to relieve some of the pressure, yet at the same time dug her hands in his buttocks to press him closer, pushing up with her hips until they were mashed tight and every fraction of him was pounding inside.

They both made sounds. Glenn clutched at her and began to pant as his strong body arched and bowed, ravishing her fast and hard and deep. Jessie responded by pumping her stretched loins in quick matching tempo—*quick*, like a maddened rabbit, like a dog in heat, furiously intent on only one thing—the orgasm, the release of bliss, the eruption of the sensations spiraling to their peak.

Glenn pummeled her with intensifying fury, his meaty staff swelling to greater size. Jessie was jolted by his thrusts, each one like an electric bomb exploding in her belly. She gasped and cried out and climaxed again in a blaze of violent delight. Her pelvis arched up, grinding as Glenn shivered, spasmed, and volcanoed his spewing eruption deep into the squeezing recesses of her loins.

Drained of energy yet sensually alive, Jessie let her bent legs slide down limply on either side of Glenn. He dropped forward, remaining locked between her pulsating thighs. Satiated, contentedly entwined, they listened to the fading rain and grumbling thunder, dozing off while the storm receded into the distance.

Sometime later Glenn withdrew and quietly departed. Jessie did not know when, but sensed the loss before returning to sleep.

Sometime toward dawn, she foggily heard Dwight arrive.

Sometime after that, Glenn snuck back in with a finger to his lips. Again they made love, savoring each fresh touch of their naked flesh, knowing they were being foolish for risking sex here and now and relishing it all the more because of it. And again he left, this time because the housekeeper was expected pretty soon.

In the first blush of a serene, fiery morning, they

dressed and rejoined out on the wide veranda that over-looked the central well and main ranch trail. Brick and Jackson were already gone, but Jessie and Glenn chatted softly in order not to awaken Dwight or his nighthawk partner, Big Fletcher, who was asleep in the bunkhouse. The housekeeper was starting to serve them breakfast when they spotted Ki arriving on the trail at an easy jog.

Exchanging greetings, Ki walked his pinto to the stable barn while the housekeeper bustled to set another place. When Ki came and sat down, he took a close look at Jessie's satsified countenance and decided not to ask if her visit had been interesting.

Glenn told him anyway. "You missed a lot of excitement last night, Ki. Gunnies sneak-attacked during the storm, and it was touch'n go afore we fought 'em off. Jessie don't think they're Nehalem men, and I kinda string with her. They're plain owlhooters."

"Strange," Ki replied thoughtfully, and he recounted the capture of Froggy Tode and the fears of Quentin Pollard. "That lawyer has the guts of a gnat, or else has some reason for putting in a word for Tode. Despite it, everyone's convinced Tode is behind all the outlawry, but he was behind jail bars when you were struck. So he may be a boss, but it's doubtful he can be the boss in charge."

Jessie nodded. "Likely not, Ki. A gang losing its head acts that way, scattering, maybe making a grab-and-run. But the raid was to hit the Box L and have us hit back at Nehalem, which might've worked if we and the crew hadn't happened to be on hand. Point is, though, it was part of a long-range scheme needing direction, someone in firm control. Tode couldn't be, and I can't believe Pollard capable of it, although his actions do seem a bit suspect."

"It ain't so odd for Pollard to be scared of retaliation," Glenn countered. "And he's never had dealings with Tode. Avoids him and most everybody 'cept for Doc Augustas, who's more on his level."

Ki looked sardonic. "We saw his pamphlet. You buy it?"

"Well, him and the doc have a way of making a feller swallow anything as gospel, no matter how loco sounding." Glenn squirmed. "I ain't so sure now as before. The doc treated Pa's gunshot, and the wound healed, but Pa was slunk in a stupor most all the time. After he died, the doc sent us a big bill that near killed us, too."

Casually Jessie asked, "Where's the sanatorium?"

"Oh, north a ways, 'twixt us and town. It's on the nice side of some high ground bordering a stretch of Nehalem's spread, which doglegs up around us from the south and west. You want to go?"

"Just curious." Jessie shrugged. "Actually, I think we ought to ride into town and report the raid to Sheriff Renwick."

"Not me. I'm on day duty, and it'd be a fat waste of time and hossflesh to boot," Glenn objected bitterly. "The sheriff moseyed through his motions when Pa got shot, didn't find a clue, and left warning us not to slander Nehalem. Now, if it'd been Nehalem shot, he'd have done anything to dig the killer out."

"Maybe," Jessie allowed, "but he has his troubles too, and I've a notion he's good at heart. Worth a try, I feel."

Ki, finishing his ham and eggs, remarked, "I'd like a stab at tracking those raiders. The storm would've washed out normal prints, but I bet they chewed up plenty of mud on their getaway."

"I'll take you to the canyon," Glenn offered, "show you where, and introduce you to the crew so you won't get beaned by mistake."

"Thanks. Before we head out, we do have time for seconds, don't we?" Smiling, Ki handed his empty plate to the housekeeper, who was standing by his side and marveling at his capacity.

Chapter 7

Shortly, as Ki and Glenn were departing, Jessie rode off toward town on a buckskin gelding, her pick of the Box L saddle stock.

After some miles she cut from the trail. While the sun rose hotter, she struck cross-country to tawny hillocks that jutted like teeth of a blunt saw. Nearing, she came upon a thin, rarely used path that wound generally in the same direction, so she took it, quickening her pace, until it joined a larger wagon lane that curved in from the East and continued on into the hills. The lane led her another couple of miles to a fork, and in the middle of the fork was a sign with an arrow pointing left that read:

DR. AUGUSTAS' SANATORIUM OF DISTINCTION

Heartened, Jessie angled leftward. She was off the trail again and forging her own route up sandy banks, over stony gulches, and through patches of briar and bear grass. Eventually she topped a final ridge. The downslope ahead was not too steep and dropped to a deep, sheltered pocket in which enough trees and brush were thriving to indicate it was supported by a pretty fair water table.

There, surrounded by tamarack and wildflower-speckled grasses, Jessie saw the sanatorium. She loosened the cinch on the buckskin, ground-reined it in shade to graze, then took the field glasses from her canvas bag, which she'd brought along in case she stayed over in town. She settled in shadow and focused her glasses on the sanatorium.

The main building was a converted ranch house, formerly the Kessler home, and had a long veranda running around three sides. It showed where additions and enlargings had been done, and one recently attached wing had iron bars cemented in the adobe frames of its small windows. There was also a carnival tent rigged near four brown sulfur springs, from which rank fumes wafted in the morning air. Darker yet less noxious smoke trickled from the fires of the many cabins and smaller tents that dotted the rolling grounds on the opposite side of the hacienda.

For a good hour, Jessie relaxed on the ridge, observing. In that time she saw men and women she could tell were patients. Some were in dressing gowns, reclining in deck chairs or lying in the sun or bathing in the silty hot springs. She surmised that others in white pants and shirts were male attendants, and that the few who were visible in the open kitchen doorway were cooks. Occasionally she noticed activity around the stable and corrals, the corncrib, storehouses and other sheds, but she never caught sight of Augustas himself. He probably remained inside where he kept his thumb, so to speak, on the pulse of things. He couldn't have strayed very far, she concluded; nobody could have—the entire outfit and immediate acreage were encircled by gleaming, three-strand barbed wire fencing.

It was approaching noon when she decided to pack it in. She checked the trails in sight and the lay of the land before she recinched her horse and worked back down to the fork. From there she loped eastward along the dusty lane and past where she'd entered earlier on the path, keeping a wary eye peeled for dust plumes of oncoming riders. She saw no one until the lane intersected the formal main road that headed south into Elbow—the same road, in fact, that she and Ki had first taken to reach the town; but then, in their hurry, they had overlooked the sign that pointed to the sanatorium.

She turned townward. It lay distant like a black, shimmery blotch. The sun was at its zenith and heat waves radiated off the land. When Jessie glimpsed a band of riders far ahead come dropping from the foothills, it was just a blur of vague shadows against the blinding backdrop. They vanished into town, and she thought nothing more about it until she heard gunfire from there.

Alarmed, Jessie urged her buckskin into a gallop, hoofbeats lifting the dry and powdery dust in roiling clouds behind her. Elbow grew more distinct and the gunshots more pernicious. She rushed through the ragged outskirts and into the main street. Now she could discern ahead many riders and dismounted figures close to the law office. The office was dark, but from its front window the flame of a shotgun showed that someone in there was fighting. She noted that among the shots and hoarse shouts and shriller voices of frightened women was an ominous hard thudding, low and rhythmic.

It took Jessie a second to make the connection; then with lashing reins, she veered her horse sidelong and around back of the buildings. Sure enough, at the rear of the law office was a knot of men who drew back in unison and then drove forward together, again and again. They had a heavy log with which they were smashing through the adobe jail wall. The defender, whom Jessie assumed to be Sheriff Renwick, could not cover all sides, and bullets riddled whichever window he tried to fire from.

As Jessie, her pistol drawn, charged on, she saw the attackers throw down their battering ram and saw the black hole they had punched in the jail wall. Several of them reached over the pile of rubble and helped Froggy Tode out, hastening him to their waiting horses.

There was a brief gunfight at the breach as the man inside attempted to stop his prisoner's escape. His shotgun roared again, but after an answering salvo from the enemy, it fell silent.

Now Jessie raised her Colt to trigger into the massing gunmen, but some were watching for just such interference. She saw orange-red flames of spurting revolvers turned her way as they tore around to cover her. The bulk of saddled gunmen started off with Tode in the other direction. The outriders then followed, linking with those who'd been attacking from the front, and riding south out of Elbow. A few townfolk had armed themselves and were shooting from behind barrels and buildings, but the town overall seemed peculiarly empty, even for midday, and resistance was too light and sporadic to prevent the breakout or flight.

It would be certain death, with no objective to achieve, if Jessie rode straight into the blazing guns of the ready outlaws. She swerved, aware that lead was too close for comfort, a slug ventilating her hat while other bullets kicked dirt near her buckskin's hooves. Dust and acrid smoke drifted over the street in the hot noon air. A hasty citizen tried for Jessie, shooting before realizing she wasn't one of the enemy. The outlaws sped on, the hooves of their horses drumming on the loose planks of the Sangrar Wash bridge. The rear guard moved slowly after to delay any pursuit. Jessie, cutting through an alley and circling the buildings, was fired upon and turned, unable to beat those last to the bridge.

"No use," she murmured, her face smudged, her pistol burning in her hand. She had scored hits, she knew. An outlaw spawled dead behind the jail and others had carried off Starbuck lead. Yet most had managed to get clean away with Froggy Tode and could lurk in wait at any point to blast anyone foolhardy enough to chase after. She swung her horse wearily back into town.

Men and some women were at the jail, a sad hush to the gathering as the body inside was collected. Rather than it being Sheriff Renwick, however, Jessie saw that they carried out a hairless codger wearing old black pants and a dirty black shirt and shoddy boots. Dismounting, she overheard a man sigh, "Pore ol' Baldy, he was a brave coot. Wish we could've done more."

"Wish there were more of us to do more," another man growled, and her puzzlement began to clear as this man called to a third, "Hi, Lansdale. Say, didn't you ride with Sheriff Renwick and the boys?"

"Naw, the sheriff didn't need my extra gun. He'd already sworn in forty guys," Lansdale replied. "Ain't nuthin' compared to the swearing he'll do when he gets back and finds his dep'ty shot and Tode gone."

"Yeah," a fourth chipped in, "that attack on the Sixty-Six must've been a trick to draw Renwick and our best fighters outta town."

"He'd never've fallen for it at night," the third said. "But it bein' broad day, and Prinzoni bein' his prime witness, well . . ."

"Well, shut up and help me cart Baldy to the mortician's. There's some carrion around, too, needing burial so it won't smell up the place." Lansdale's face was beet red. "Fellers, we've got to clean them polecats out so's we can call our souls our own."

Jessie moved away, piecing together what had happened. Prinzoni was the ranch hand Tode had tried to rob, Ki had said, and his ranch must be the Sixty-Six. Sometime this morning, Sheriff Renwick got word the Sixty-Six was under attack and jumped to the conclusion that the attackers were pals of Tode's bent on killing the witness. He'd obeyed his natural impulse, massing a posse and stampeding to the rescue—what any competent lawman might do—only to find, Jessie was sure, that the attackers had conveniently just ridden off. So he'd have done the natural thing again, picking up their fresh trail and sticking to it, while the attackers led him in circles and then headed for Elbow to jailbreak Tode. And when he and his posse eventually did return, they'd straggle in as fatigued as their horses, unable to pursue.

A slick ploy, all right, timed and executed well.

She headed for Quentin Pollard's office. She would have liked to question the attorney, but found the door locked and nobody answering her knock. "He must be out seeing this excitement," she mused, yet she could not recall having seen Pollard in the crowd at the jail.

Continuing on and feeling stymied for the moment, Jessie entered the Castle Dome for a quick snack and a breather to marshal her thoughts. The dining room was quiet and empty, a rest from last night's raucous clutter. Among the sparce crop of patrons, however, Pollard sat eating an ample meal and reading as he enjoyed his repast.

Looks like he's scared pissless, Jessie thought sarcastically as she approached. "Good day," she said. "May I join you?"

Pollard nodded affably. "Hello, Miss Starbuck, please do."

Jessie sat down, waving away the approaching waitress, while holding her other hand to her stomach. "Not hungry, I'm afraid."

"Oh? Feeling under the weather today?"

"I'm fine," she declared. "Your sheriff's the one who isn't fine, allowing himself to be lured away so Tode could break out of jail."

"A scandalous outrage, no question. Yet the plea he answered was genuine, m'dear. A Sixty-Six wrangler had been out, spotted the attack begin, and raced for town at once." Pollard sighed heavily. "Froggy is a formidable character with dangerous cohorts. He would not be daunted to sacrifice any and all of us."

"So the attack was a charade?"

Pollard's jowls waggled as he nodded. "I understand Prinzoni was first to go down. I advised him against baying

72

the hounds of the law upon Tode, but he insisted, a rash habit of youth." Pollard's husky voice dropped as he cleared his throat. "Confound cattarh, it chokes me up. Excuse me, I must sip my hourly dram of medicine." He guzzled from his tonic bottle and shoved it across to Jessie.

Jessie shook her head, making a wry, queasy face.

"My, my, you really aren't feeling very well, are you?"

"I am fine," she insisted, but then reluctantly confessed, "Truth is, I haven't been the same since a mule kicked me last year."

"Ah yes, of course. Foregoing meals won't cure you, m'dear. You should consult Doc Augustas and be properly taken care of."

"You think wallowing in mud baths will cure me?"

"Indubitably. Augustas is a great benefactor to the community and nation, and people flock to fortify their health with his hot springs and rarified minerals and patent medicines. No finer healer exists. Here, I'll write you a note to guarantee your entry."

Taking out another pamphlet, Pollard scribbled hastily: To Dr. Augustas—Sir, this will introduce Miss Jessica Starbuck, sad possessor of a troubled digestion. For my as for her sake, treat her well—Quentin. He passed it to Jessie.

Jessie grasped it. "Oh, I can't wait to be cured."

"An impatient patient," Pollard quipped. "I wish your luck in your quest for precious health, m'dear. Are you leaving already?"

"Yes, sir," Jessie said, standing. "And thanks again."

Slightly hunched over and with a pained expression, she limped from the dining room. Soon she was riding out of Elbow on her buckskin, heading back north toward Augustas' sanatorium.

There had never been a mule that had kicked her. There was nothing wrong with her appetite, and she could not only bite nails but digest them as well. There definitely

73

would be something bad about her stomach if the chance she was taking backfired. She felt impelled to take it, though. Her book's entry on Froggy Tode had planted seeds of doubt concerning Augustas, and since last night some remembered incidentals, insignificant in themselves, had fit together to help sprout those doubts into suspicions. Yet she had absolutely no proof she was on the right track, that Augustas was tied to Tode or to the cartel. Even supposing Augustas was, the cartel was worldwide, far-flung, very much like the many-headed Hydra of Greek mythology. Usually she rued the cartel's labyrinthine enormity, but now she was gambling that if there were a cartel head up at that sanatorium, he wouldn't know that other heads had standing orders to murder any Starbuck on sight.

But if the odds she was risking broke against her, if she lost her bet, she would very likely die after a very short illness—from a terminal case of bullet bellyache.

Chapter 8

Ki spent the morning tracing the raiders.

First, he surveyed the canyon. It had been churned to gumbo by the stampede and gunfight and now was drying under hot sunlight to a hash of illegible marks. So Ki worked on getting an overall impression, on gaining a feel for the raiders and some sense of their traits and actions, it being an axiom with him that if he knew the habits of those he was tracking, he could put himself in their position and figure out what they'd likely do. Besides, he didn't need to pick up their trail here. Glenn had told him, and their path of strewn cartridge cases proved, that the raiders had fled the way they'd snuck in, through the lower end of the canyon. He began in earnest there, where Brick and Jackson were repairing the fence across the draw. Despite the barbed wire barrier, the draw seemed to be a natural attraction about which Ki found horse tracks, boot tracks, even some shoat tracks, and, of course, innumerable sheep tracks. Those made before the storm were mostly washed out, and those made afterward were fresh, sharply indented. Those made during the storm by the galloping raiders were unique, however, for they were not so much a set of individual prints as they were a distinctive pattern of plowed furrows and stomped holes left in the congealing, sodden ground.

Ki followed the telltale scars through the harsh sheep range west of the canyon. He lost them in the hardscrabble patches and across stony ledges and for a time trusted to keeping to the line of travel already taken. Pretty soon he came to the Box L boundary. Its line fence also was down, its wire strands no doubt clipped by the raiders. Encouraged, he crossed there onto Nehalem's spread.

For a while the land was as rough as on the Box L side. This must be some odd chunk, Ki surmised, left over from the neatly divided section sold to the Latimers, and Nehalem was missing a bet by not putting it to similar use with sheep. He was obstinate as a jackass, but to Ki's mind he showed signs of having plenty of wrinkles on his horns; he might not be adverse to listening to reason, if it sounded as though money were doing the talking.

Gradually the terrain changed; fertile meadows now stretching between the scraps and gullies. The raiders kept to the rocks, their tracks becoming scarcer and forcing Ki to deduce much of their course. It wasn't instinct; he wasn't a bloodhound; it was solid logic and long experience, confirmed by an occasional imprint or other sign. Around him he saw an increasing number of fawn Guernseys and larger black-and-white Holsteins, sleek and healthy, roaming the growing pastures. The skirting raider trail led up onto the pointed end of a spearheaded-shaped plateau, sterile of growth and wedged like a stone delta over the flatland toward a yonder tier of foothills.

The tracks vanished. Painstakingly Ki guided his pinto for a mile in search of a sign. Finding none, he dismounted and walked the horse in scouring sweeps, scrutinizing the grass fringes for any indication that the raiders had dropped and struck boldly across the field. Heat lay like a suffocating weight, the sun scorching his bent back, and after a couple more miles of failure, Ki stopped to refigure his possibilities. The table had broadened considerably and continued to widen at a good ten-degree fan into the distance. Nothing ahead or on either side appeared to be menacing enough to avoid or attractive enough to head for, and there was nothing between but blank stone.

The possibilities of direction were many; the probabilities of detection were zilch.

Reluctantly giving up any thought of them now, Ki turned back for the Box L. He headed directly instead of retracting the twisted outlaw trail. He dipped his hat against the late morning glare as he cut across a field. By noon he again was in the strip bordering the Box L. Winding amid its low spurs and crevices, he chanced to enter a notch where rain had collected in a low, tublike boulder.

Drawing up, he noticed that something else was heading toward the Box L line. It was too far south and too hidden to be seen, but whatever it was, it was strange enough to the country to send swallows protesting in the air. His pinto tugged at the rein, seeking the puddle, and Ki sat for a long moment while she drank, concentrating on solving the enigma of the disturbance.

Then, although Ki heard no sound, the pinto suddenly lifted her head, her sharp ears pointing, to look southeastward where more birds were winging. This second flock struck a warning cord in Ki. He angled his horse out of the notch and up a steep hogback, his eyes taking quick stock of the terrain. To the North and East was nothing, but diagonally to his right on Box L land and due south on Nehalem land, he watched both batches of swallows trying to alight, only to rise restlessly again, seeming to be flitting on courses that were bringing them closer.

Ki descended, his last doubts evaporating. No creature of the wild would so pester those birds with its presence. And no human had ordinary business here in a remote stretch between quarreling ranches. There may be nothing to it, Ki realized, but it sure was a prime setup for an ambush.

With this in mind, Ki strove to reach the point where he estimated he would intercept. He slewed down off the hogback, his haste almost causing his horse to flounder, and was racing across a finger of rolling meadow when he caught a glimpse of the rider coming from the south. The distance was too great, the sun too dazzling, for Ki to make out features, but the rider appeared to be a small, slightly built man, exhibiting excellent horsemanship as he flogged the breeze recklessly toward the nearby Box L line.

Ki charged straight after—or at least as straight as the jagged landscape would allow. Swiftly the rider passed from view. Ki rode on, chasing at a tangent that brought him diving into a culvert. He followed the culvert to its end and traversed a chain of eroded, rubble-strewn clefts and outcrops, his route growing more clogged and hazardous with each step the pinto made.

It took him longer than he wished or expected it would, but finally Ki halted at the base of a slope dotted with parched bushes. The critical spot, Ki judged, was liable to be on or just over the top of the slope. It was only a few hundred feet high, but he'd have to go on foot; the horse would create too much noise.

He ground-hobbled his pinto in a shady nook, drew a dagger that he clenched between his teeth, and started up through the low brush. Despite his sense of urgency, he climbed cautiously, gauging the baked, storm-scrubbed rock and meager vegetation. He heard nothing and wondered if that meant he was in time or too late, if something other than an ambush was being connived. When he mounted the slope, he allowed only his head to show above the crest. He scanned the land around and below, sun burning his eyes and heat making sweat trickle down into them and sting.

The far side slanted to a narrow gully, which was akin to a horse path snaking along the base of the slope and off again among the broken rises and scrubby growth. A short way from it was a scooped little pocket whose floor, as yet, Ki could not see. Like a row of snaggled teeth, clumped boulders shut in three sides of the pocket. The fourth side, the low side, was screened instead by some scrawny trees and a tangled thicket, whose inedible greenery was being gnawed upon by two staked-out horses.

Ki eased over the rounded crest and began creeping down toward the pocket. He didn't feel relieved one whit by seeing that an ambush was not in the offing; a secret confab stunk different but as foul. Treachery, a sell-out by somebody from one of the spreads, loomed in Ki's mind. Yet when he crept to the shoulder of the nearest boulder, he thought perhaps he hadn't been so far off about an ambush —if this weren't a trap, then certainly there was a falling-out between conspirators going on, for he could discern their savage grunts and agonized gasps and frantic thrashings about on the ground as they wrangled in mortal hand-to-hand combat.

Quickening, Ki slid along the curve of the boulders until he came to a crevice scarcely wide enough to squeeze through. He ducked in, worming between compacted boulders to a position behind a hedge of stones. One brief peek into the pocket told Ki he had come to the right place, okay . . . but at the wrong time.

Most definitely at the wrong time.

A nude young couple was locked in carnal embrace. The youth lay squirming on his back, arching his pelvis in stabbing concert while the girl squatted atop with her hips bucking gently, then swiftly, more slowly, faster. He was panting and groaning, his chestnut hair damp from his exertions, his brown eyes feverish with the exuberance a male in his early twenties has toward sex. He'd have to be the Box L rider, Ki knew, since no female other than Jessie was staying there; and though his expression was contorted by lust, his features were too similar to Glenn Latimer's for Ki not to identify him as brother Dwight.

So obviously the girl had to be the rider from the south. Ki didn't recognize her, but he recalled the Castle Dome fight between Glenn and Uriah Nehalem and decided she must be one of Nehalem's twin daughters. She was riding Dwight harder than she had any horse, moaning while pistoning astraddle his upthrusting loins. She kept twisting her nubile torso from side to side as if straining to screw herself deeper upon him, whipping her long braids of wheat-blond hair and giving Ki a glimpse of bobbing breasts and a pert gamin face, snub-nosed and blue-eyed. She was eighteen or nineteen, no more than twenty; yet whatever her age, Ki figured he was watching an expert in the art, for the woman at whose bare ass he was staring was carefully regulating the pace.

Ki withdrew fast before he was discovered by the lovers. Resheathing his dagger, he backed from the boulders and silently hastened up and over the slope. He took it easier then, returning to his horse, mounting, and slowly working his way to the gully and back around near the pocket. Their horses were still there, to no surprise. He picketed the pinto and lolled in the shade, trying to ignore the giggles, the squeals, the bellows and screeches, while he waited for a more opportune time to make his appearance.

At long last Ki detected different sounds, the welcome sounds of creaking saddle leather and jangling bridle irons. Remounting, he approached the pocket at a saunter, acting normal and none too quiet, his pinto's shoes clicking dully on the hard surface.

Even so, his arrival startled the couple as they were readying to depart. Now dressed primly in an ankle-length dress, the girl stood rigid with a paling face dominated by fear-misted eyes. Dwight, clad in shirt and jeans, reared from cinching his saddle to stare with bulging eyes and sagging jaw.

"W—who're you and whaddyuh want?" he stammered.

The corners of Ki's mouth quirked. "My name's Ki."

"Ki? Then you're . . ." Dwight heaved a sigh. "We ain't met, Ki, but my brother told me about you. I'm Dwight

Latimer. This's Miss Nehalem, Hope Nehalem." He turned to the girl. "I told you what Glenn told me, remember? Ki sides the Starbuck lady."

Hope glared at Ki, the fear in her eyes replaced by flint. "That doesn't give you the right to steal up on people and scare them half out of their wits. What do you think you're doing here, anyway?"

"Saw your horses." Ki explained he'd been tracking the raiders, lost them, and was returning to the Box L. He left it at that.

"There, Hope, now simmer down." Dwight looked surprised. "Y'see, Ki, for a second we thought her pa had set you—well, somebody—to keep a watch on her. Maybe slit my gizzard as well."

Hope nodded, temper calming. "Please don't tell a soul."

"Upon my word, nary a word." Ki regarded her face and then Dwight's and abruptly he smiled. Their romp here was for more than to scratch an itch; it was apparent in their tones, their glances, their support for each other that they felt in love. "Don't worry, I promise. But it's a pip, the sheepman sparking the cowman's daughter."

Dwight grinned abashedly and scuffed a boot in the dirt. Hope's eyes widened more, and now it was neither fear nor indignation in them, but defiance. "Is that so terrible?" she demanded.

"Terrible!" Ki chuckled. "It's a case of the worse it is, the better it is. Just flirting has your father pawing sod, but you get serious enough, and he'll cool down after a spell. He'll have to."

"I wonder," Dwight said resignedly. "Of late it's all been going awful bad, and you'n Miz Starbuck are the last ruination of me'n Glenn, but somehow or another I feel better since you came."

"It'll get better, too," Ki predicted. "And I've a notion things will work out for you and Glenn and work out well for Uriah at the same time. By the way, Miss Nehalem, how is he recovering?"

"I don't know, Mr. Ki. I haven't seen him today."

"Ki, plain Ki. I suppose he slept in late. Good."

"Fair's fair, so call me Hope," she replied with a curtsy. "No, Dad hasn't been home. Dwight informed me of Dad's holdup and being knocked out, and I well imagine he's resting over in Elbow."

The smile left Ki's eyes and his mouth tightened. "Hope, I personally saw your father leave town afterward. He was riding for home."

"Oh, you're mistaken. He likely went out for air."

"Your father was in no mood to ramble around. He was in no shape to go alone, perhaps, but couldn't have been stopped. He might've passed out on the way, or had an accident, or may have been . . ." Ki paused, reluctant to vent his worst fears.

She gave a low, gasping cry. "I must get back!"

"I'll come with you," Ki said gravely. "I want to find your father. Don't shake your head at me. It's important, I know."

"Hope, I wish I could be along, too. You know if I were caught on your pa's spread, I'd be blasted so full of holes, I'd starve to death from leakin' my victuals out." Dwight clasped the girl's trembling hand. "So take Ki in my stead. If half the stuff Glenn told me is true, Ki can locate your pa if anyone can, safe and sound."

She sighed. "Very well. He did find us, after all."

"I'll ride ahead," Ki said. "Your good-byes don't need me."

"I'll catch up before the gully ends," Hope pledged.

Ki nodded, smiled at both, and turned his pinto downslope.

After a mile of gully, Ki traveled south another two miles before hearing the gallop of hooves behind him. He glanced back, saw Hope Nehalem spurring after him, and reined in to wait. When she pulled abreast, they continued on together at a lope.

She looked as if her delay had been worth it, but she apologized and then asked with innocence, "Did you happen by us any earlier?"

Ki too was innocent. "No, not me. Why?"

"Oh, nothing. I guess it looked rather funny to you," she remarked demurely, "but it's the only way we have to see each other. Dwight and I met soon after he moved here and, well, things sort of developed, and for some while we've been getting together there at noon two, three times a week. We never dreamed we'd be discovered."

"I won't blab. I'm just sorry I gave you such a start."

"Forget it, I have, I . . . I'm much more frightened about Dad." Her lips quivered and anguish now etched her expression, but her luminous blue eyes flared with resolve. "We must find him, Ki, we must. If he's disappeared, if he's been kidnapped or m—murdered . . ."

"Now you're scaring yourself, Hope. We will find him."

"I'm not scared for me, but for Dwight. And for Glenn, too. Because if anything has befallen Dad, they'll be blamed. Don't you see? Our crewhands are good at heart, but they're loyal to a fault and already chafed raw and ugly mean. The Latimers and everyone connected with the Box L—yes, including you and Miss Starbuck—will be marked for vengeance, guilty or not; all of you will be targets for death."

Chapter 9

When Jessie reached her destination, the gates stood open beneath a banner entrance sign that read:

DR. AUGUSTAS' SANATORIUM OF DISTINCTION
BYRON AUGUSTAS, M. D., PROP.

Her way in was blocked, though, by a couple of heavy-set men who came ambling from an open wayside shed. They wore soiled white pants and shirts, toted carbines out of habit more than caution, and wasted no politeness on a female who dressed man-style and rode man-style. Real ladies didn't do such, however pretty they were.

The stouter guard demanded, "State your business."

"I'm here to see Doc Augustas."

The other guard smirked. "He don't treat social diseases."

"Your problem, not mine," Jessie retorted. "Let me by."

The first guard snickered, which further provoked his partner. "Listen, toots, the doc ain't paid in trade, just in cash, and he don't need no more honeybees to service needs here. So buzz off."

"Not till I consult the doctor." Jessie took the folded pamphlet from her pocket and handed it to the first guard. "This's a note to him from Quentin Pollard, who swears the doctor will be able to cure me."

"Well, whyn't you say so?" The guard whistled shrilly, and a boy came dashing from the main building. "Show the, uh, lady to the office, and give this note to the doc," the guard ordered.

Jessie passed the gate and followed the boy to the big house, where she hitched her horse at a post, stepped to the front porch, and walked inside as the boy held the door. The broad foyer was like the connecting bar of the letter H, with corridors branching front and back and to the left and right. In the middle was a curved staircase that swept to the second floor. At the rear, where the boy was going, was an oversized mahogany door with a gold-leaf sign: OFFICE.

The boy gestured for her to wait and went in with her note. Jessie gazed about, idly wondering how many zillion mud baths and tonics were sold to pay for all this swank. The boy emerged and signaled to her, so she entered the office. It was actually more of an anteroom with a door on each side and a prominent three-piece set of sofa, loveseat, and chair. But there was one office desk at which sat a haughty man in a gray worsted suit.

"Have a seat, ma'am. The doctor will see you soon."

Soon turned out to be forty minutes later. Then a speaking tube by the desk blew a flatulent note; the man answered it, listened, and hooked it back. "Please go in, ma'am. The door to your left."

Jessie shuffled through the door and closed it behind her. Immediately the odor common to medical chambers—drugs, antiseptics, chemicals—stung her nostrils. The office itself was carpeted and well lighted with thick green drapes roped back from doors overlooking a sunny back yard. In front of her was an imposing desk of oak and rosewood, but peripherally she saw a high examination couch, some forceps and similar instruments, and cabinets of bottles, boxes, and textbooks. In a far corner her startled glance encountered a skeleton suspended by a silver wire.

It was the small man behind the great desk, however, that held Jessie's attention. Byron Augustas was as dressed to the hilt as he'd been last night: black frock coat on despite the heat, a white stock at his throat. Then, however, he'd been intense with concern for a stricken patient. Now, relaxed, smile lines radiated from wise old eyes that beamed such trust, such virtue, such benevolence that his face appeared almost cherubic.

"A good afternoon to you," he greeted her warmly. "Your name is Miss Jessica Starbuck, according to Mr. Pollard's note. Would you perchance be related to the Starbuck family in Texas?"

"Close blood kin," Jessie replied. "Yes, sir."

"How fortunate for you. Now, Mr. Pollard merely wrote that you have troubled digestion. Could you be more specific?"

"Well, ever since a mule kicked me last year, I've felt generally indisposed in that region." Her tone was aggrieved, but bravely so. "I'm peaked from lack of appetite, bouts of wind colic and the sore bloats, and a cramping up till at times I can't sleep."

"Yes, a classic injury...Just lie on my table, if you would...Loosen your blouse and trousers. That's fine. Ah..."

Jessie stretched flat on the examination couch, midriff bared from breasts to crotch. Augustas, to his credit, never strayed out of bounds while probing her with his strong, agile fingers.

"Does it hurt here? No? There? Yes, and over here?"

"Oww," Jessie moaned, flinching. "Oh. Ouch!"

Augustas frowned, stepped back. "More acute than I thought. Miss Starbuck, you suffer the maladies you mentioned. Plus morbid dyspepsia, torpid liver, and serious internal malfunctionings."

"My, that sounds perfectly dreadful."

"You'll need massages and soothing hot springs and frequent application of mud balm concentrate. A strict diet besides, and medicines I will prescribe. We may yet have to apply leeches. I cannot emphasise too strongly the gravity of your condition."

Jessie gasped. "Is it . . . fatal?"

Augustas didn't respond at once, but went and puffed into his speaking tube. The door opened and the man stuck his head in, sending Jessie scrambling to dress. Augustas told him, "Miss Starbuck will require a room for the next two weeks, preferably near the mud baths."

"Yes, sir. Ma'am, is the buckskin your horse?"

Jessie nodded.

The man ducked out, shutting the door. Augustas turned to Jessie again, smiling reassuringly. "To answer you, simply follow my corrective regimen carefully and conscientiously, and I foresee no reason you shouldn't recover. Now, room and board, my fee, medicines . . . An even two hundred a week, I think will suffice."

"Good health is never too expensive," Jessie declared, and peeled fifty dollars from bills she kept tucked away. "This is a down payment. I'll arrange a transfer of funds tomorrow."

"As you wish. Starbuck credit is good as gold." Augustas returned to his desk. "My receptionist will get you settled in and bring your medicines this evening. Good day, Miss Starbuck."

A hulluva slick charlatan, Jessie thought as she left, as smooth as the mud he peddles. If she didn't know she was fit, she'd swear she was on death's door. She may be yet, staying here.

The young man in the anteroom said, "I'm Tyrone, ma'am, and I'll handle all your appointments and necessities. I've taken the liberty of having your horse stabled, and your bag will be brought shortly to your room, ten in the B wing. Please come with me."

Jessie trailed Tyrone out into the foyer. They were angling toward a side corridor when they were stopped by a thin elderly man, white of hair and with an ailing face and a chronic rasp. Buttonholing Tyrone, the old man croaked out, "You tell the sawbones I'm gonna see him tonight, boy. Tell him I'm convinced I'm doing right."

"I will, Mr. Muldow. I'm sure he's already aware."

"Aware him agin. I ain't got time to lollygag."

Moving on, they went along the corridor to the B wing. The wing smelled peculiarly of clay, soap, and ether—and for that matter, so did her room, which was otherwise pleasant and comfortable. By then Tyrone had run out of regulations to spout and departed.

Jessie left her room as soon as her bag was delivered and wandered slowly through the fenced grounds, maintaining her invalid's pose. She had no trouble blending in with the self-engrossed manner of other patients hooked by Augustas' publicity. Many were dowagers and matrons taken with the vapors and feminine complaints. Some women, though, showed signs of hard saloon living, and enough fit the mouthy guard's reference to honeybees to have stocked a Cheyenne cathouse. The men were either oldsters like Mr. Muldow, wasting away in sickness, or flabby husbands of the matrons, casting eyes at the honeybees, or shady gents beyond the fringes of the law. This criminal element didn't look any different, especially when sunk to the eyeballs in mud, but they had a disparity that Jessie sensed from her long experience at running such types to ground. Those who clearly were roughneck thugs all seemed to be wearing the white outfits of attendants.

"I should've figured a setup like this," she murmured.

The physical layout of the sanatorium was as she had observed it through her glasses from the hill during her first visit. Learning nothing new, other than the big tent served as the dining hall, she decided to concentrate on the main building. She went back inside to tour the ground floor casually, but whenever the opportunity arose, she glided warily through doors, pausing before opening each one to assure herself of unobserved passage. The majority were locked or occupied, their interesting secrets having to wait. She poked around in the gloom of those she could enter, searching drawers and cabinets, crates and containers, finding lots of stuff without unearthing the slightest shred of useful information.

Eventually she came to the recently added wing that had the small, barred windows. It abutted the old house where a library had been—and still was to a great extent, most of the furnishings and bookcases remaining intact, though now a connecting doorway and a paneled partition replaced the original end wall. By the door sat a husky attendant, his shirt bulging with a poorly concealed shoulder holster, his eyes having a droopy watchfulness, bored yet awake.

Frustrated and curious, Jessie retreated before the guard noticed her and headed outside again. The perimeter of the building was not formally gardened, but did have some bordering hedges and flower bushes that she dutifully admired while strolling alongside the wing, trying not to act nosy or arouse suspicions. There were numerous alert attendants about, and one was turning her way even now, as she glanced at the barred windows, three of them in a row.

Came a low whisper: "Help."

For a second, the murky image of a man's face pressed against the iron bars of the middle window. Jessie caught a glimpse of his pleading eyes; then he vanished abruptly as though collapsing or being snatched violently back. Instantly she angled away, aware of the danger, jolted by his flash of desperation, and shocked by her flash of recognition. The man was Uriah Nehalem; he couldn't be here, caged behind bars, yet she was positive he's whom she saw.

The next moment, while thinking of reasons he would have been taken captive, Jessie chastised herself: "Damn, I should've considered a possibility like this, too!" And she realized that although this complicated her plans, compounded her peril and chances of failure, she had to try to

89

rescue Nehalem—somehow and soon.

The balance of the afternoon Jessie spent figuring ways and means. She couldn't attack openly or even count on intimidating with her few weapons, for Augustas had overwhelming power and organization. So she'd have to be sneaky. After dusk was best for stealth, when vision was distorted and the sanatorium would be lulled by eventide, its patients retiring, its attendants off duty and replaced by a smaller crew of night sentries.

Nor could she slip away for help. Wherever she raised it—the Box L, Nehalem's spread, a sheriff's posse— they'd never smash past the gates and into the fortified wing before Augustas could kill Nehalem and escape. And she would lose what advantage she'd gained by her infiltrating. So she'd have to get Nehalem out, and the only way was through the door. Covertly watching the guard from a corridor cubby, Jessie was able after a long while to determine his rather lax schedule. Every half hour or so he made the rounds of the wing and an adjacent section of halls and rooms, returning in five to seven minutes to his post. She hoped that the night shift kept the same routine.

Nor could Jessie count on swiping a horse, not even her own buckskin. Assuming the horse kept quiet, the rest of the stable would surely snort up a fuss. Besides, it would be impossible to rush the guarded main gate or to cut a hole for passage in the triple-strand barbed wire fence. So she'd have to strike on foot, and Nehalem would have to make his getaway on foot. In five to seven minutes. Furtively, without causing any alarm.

The sun continued its slow decline, slanting rays burnishing the sandy landscape, setting the western sides of buildings afire. By the time the supper bell clanged, Jessie had developed a scheme of sorts and a rash of vague apprehensions. The meal was palatable and wholesome enough, but she picked at her food, appetite squelched by her anxiety to get this fray over with as quickly as possible.

Chapter 10

After dinner, Jessie returned to her room where she waited for the last blood of the sunset to wash from the horizon.

She spent the time getting organized. With thorough care she kneaded her boots with wax preservative, which was not designed to produce a polish but to render the leather pliable and less likely to squeak. Her long hair she bound back in tight coils. She could not risk being seen traipsing about with her holster and cartridge belt, so she stowed spare shells here and there in her pockets and thrust her Colt pistol in her belt and under her shirt. She also carried a straight razor, which was easily concealed and in many aspects was deadlier than a knife.

Shadows were lengthening and the light was none too good in the hallway as Jessie checked the immediate vicinity and found it clear. She slipped out and along the hall to the foyer, pausing there and listening sharply before padding up and around to the corridor that led to Nehalem's wing. Moving on, she came to Augustas' private dining room, which was about midway and on her right. Its doors were slid wide open, and from within she could hear the clatter of dishes and the humming of a maid. She eased by the doorway, tiptoeing warily, scarcely daring to breathe until she had again ducked into the convenient cubby within view of the guard.

It was a different man, bigger and uglier. Jessie could just make him out, tilted back in his chair next to the door and reading a popular weekly. She waited, crouching motionless. Her legs were aching with cramps and her left arm had gone to sleep by the time the guard stretched, yawned, and departed on his rounds.

Gritting her teeth, Jessie forced her tortured muscles into a dash across the library. She leaned against the thick wooden door, gently turning the knob and gratified to find it wasn't locked. Cautiously she opened the door. A hinge creaked. The servant in the dining room hesitated, and for a long moment there was a nerve-racking silence . . . Then the servant pursued her aimless humming, and Jessie ducked into the wing and pressed the door closed.

She hurried down the corridor. It was dim, stubby, and lined on each side by three doors that were hinged by iron pegs and secured by sliding bars. The window in which she had glimpsed Nehalem corresponded with the middle door on her right, but from some of the others Jessie could hear faint shufflings and groans. Another time, another place, she might've considered releasing these victims, too, but not now, not with only five minutes left. Even if they were in shape to go, she couldn't have mustered them or led them to safety; they stood a much greater chance of dying during an escape than they did by staying put a while longer.

She pushed back the crossbar and pulled open the door. Stepping inside and peering into the gloom, she perceived the vague outline of a man on a cot. "Nehalem?" she whispered, approaching. "Uriah?"

"Miz Starbuck? Hot dang, I thought I seen you."

"More important, I saw you." She now saw his face was cut and bruised, his head bandage caked with dried blood. His wrists and ankles were looped tightly with rawhide thongs, which then were stretched and tied to the corners of the cot, holding him helpless. Well, not quite, she thought; he'd managed for an instant to lift bed and all to the window, before losing his balance and crashing backward. She whipped out her razor, snicked open its blade, and began slicing his bonds. "How and why did you wind up in here?"

"At gunpoint—four polecats jumping me on m'ride home. Why, I dunno. When I'd ask, they'd work me over some. P'raps that holdup gang fears I tabbed the robber who ran off, or else the Latimers pulled it so I can't protect my spread and daughters from 'em." His hands freed, Nehalem clumsily rubbed his numb wrists while Jessie parted the thongs at his ankles. "I reckon, though, Doc Augustas must plain be a quack to've been bought off and penned me in here."

Jessie agreed, but realized Nehalem could think only of motives that hit him personally. He couldn't imagine a more encompassing, more sinister plot beneath the surface events. She did not explain, although as she helped him to his feet she briefly sketched the situation here and her desire to remain and pin Augustas before he could squirm away. "So you'll have to fly the coop alone on foot, I'm afraid."

"Miz Starbuck, I think you're loony, but I won't argue. You won't be stuck here long 'nuff to get in hazard anyhow 'cause the dander I'm in I'll outpace any horse and be back in a thrice with half the valley. We'll tear this joint down 'round that humbug's ears."

A quick peek into the corridor and then they were out and rebolting the cell door. Hastening, they reached the door to the library and paused to listen, Jessie bothered by trepidation, even though they heard nothing. That was what worried her—not being able to hear or to see anything of the room beyond through the thick door. Softly, softly, she turned the knob until the latch clicked free.

She hesitated and whispered, "The guard shouldn't be back yet, but that's based on the previous guard's routine, and his might be shorter or he may've sloughed off to return early. Or someone else could've entered in his absence. Probably the room's empty, but . . ."

"Crack the door and check," Nehalem muttered.

"It has a bad hinge. The squeak will warn anybody."

"Can't risk that. Better to just go in fast and surprise."

With a swift motion, Jessie opened the door and darted into the room. The hinge squawked like a strangling crow. Nehalem took one step, lurched against the frame, and thumped to his knees, his legs still rubbery from their long constriction and buckling unexpectedly under him. And the guard, who was stooping for his paper, looked around. In a flash, he reared upright and leaped at Jessie, a startled yet determined glare in his eyes as he clawed for his shoulder holster.

Jessie did not try for her concealed pistol. She wanted to avoid gunplay, and besides, there wasn't time to draw. She made a wide swipe for the nearest handy object, a large porcelain vase on a table, and without bothering to remove its flowers, hefted and flung it overhand. Her pitch was true. The vase caught the guard solidly on the side of the head and shattered.

The man staggered, but he was nonetheless able to close the short distance and grab Jessie by the throat. "Try'n clobber me, willyuh?" he growled, his grip tightening on her neck. Frantically she struggled back, fingers stabbing for his eyes, nails like talons slashing flesh, legs hooking and trying to lock about his in order to bring him down, to make him fall so she could break free.

"Naw, yuh don't," he snarled. "Crap, naw—"

Then abruptly he slipped. The water from the broken flower vase had slopped all over the floor, and now, as they wrestled, the slick soles of his worn boots slithered in the puddle. He tumbled in a sprawling heap, bringing Jessie down on top of him. His head struck one of the projecting claw feet of the table; he grunted heavily and lay still, a dark stain oozing beneath his head.

"That blew it," Jessie gasped raggedly, as Nehalem

came and helped her regain her feet. "We raised enough rumpus to—"

"To wake the dead," he interrupted impatiently. "Who knows? We might pull out of this yet. But if there's trouble, leave me."

"I won't—"

"No sense us both gettin' caught. Nobody'd be left then to get anybody out again." Licking a dry tongue over his cracked lips, Nehalem lumbered frenetically toward the hall, fists clenched ready.

There was trouble.

Nehalem got as far as the cranny, Jessie catching up but still a few paces behind, when from the foyer stormed a bruiser of an attendant. The men charged and clashed at the dining room entrance. Nehalem with his longer arms struck first, a straight knuckler crunching against cheekbone. The attendant staggered backward, rebounded off the wall, and plunged forward again to catch a punch in the windpipe. But his momentum carried him on to pin Nehalem against a door, while his meaty hams bludgeoned chest and belly.

Jessie, her shirt loosened and with her pistol in hand, wasn't sure how or if she should intervene. Though Nehalem was being hammered into oblivion, he seemed impervious to pain, implacable with bitter rage and resentment. And now his big fists went to work, ramming, crushing, beating upon the attendant's ribs, chin, nose, eye sockets, and brow. And his knee shoved upward into the groin. The attendant ceased hitting him and doubled, retreating and dripping blood to the floor. A mistake. Nehalem's punch came up from far below and splintered his jaw.

As the attendant dropped ass over heels, there grew from the foyer a discord of running steps and riling shouts. Desperate, Jessie and Nehalem swerved into the dining room, through the far archway, and past the serving pantry, racing to locate the kitchen with a hoped-for rear exit. They reached a short area that had shelves along one side, a narrow rear staircase on the other, and a swinging door.

Nehalem forged for the door like a human dreadnought. He was about to shove it open and steam on when it swung inward, and they were confronted by a pack of armed and grimacing brutes.

The men grimaced at their victims, of course. But partly they grimaced because they couldn't squeeze through the doorway all at once, though they were trying to and were wedged tight for that initial instant. Nehalem never broke stride. He stiff-armed the door shut and added his shoulder for extra measure, thus catapulting the men backward into the kitchen with a tumultuous detonation of crashes.

"Move!" he yelled at Jessie. "I can't stall 'em forever!"

Regrouping, the men smacked the door and sheared it clean off its hinges. Nehalem danced aside at the last moment, and the men soared through unchecked, careening as the door panel caught underfoot and then tripping and tumbling ungainly. Nehalem booted one in passing and followed with a body blow to the chest of another. A third caught a kick from Jessie that sent him sprawling.

This had the makings of a royal donnybrook, which puzzled Jessie. By rights she and Nehalem should be riddled with lead by now, yet not a shot had been fired so far. Most of the men were wielding weapons like truncheons and bats—Nehalem caught a glancing whack on his left forearm with a sawed-off hickory limb; the arm went numb, the anger rose upon him, and his right fist knocked the offender flat. The few who brandished firearms were toting them reversed for clubbing—save for one wringy hardcase who was aiming for a target, until Jessie grabbed the barrel and rammed stock into belly; at the same time she gave the gunman a swift kick to the shin, and the revolver came away in her hands. She brained him senseless with it and then tossed it out the window by the stairs, smashing half its small panes. She wondered if for good relations a sanatorium rule was not to shoot, at least not within the main house where the moneyed patients resided. Or maybe the fighting was at such close quarters, the men simply feared hitting one another. But she had little chance to contemplate such matters, hearing the hoarse cries of the mob surging in from the dining room. And no doubt in reserve were all the awakened day attendants, probably lined up to the mud baths for a turn at getting a crack at them.

They were trapped.

"Go on, damn it, before they git a prime look at you!"

Jessie hated to. Every fiber rebelled against leaving Nehalem, though she realized he was right. She dived for the stairs, her only path of escape as the swarm came closing in from both sides with cudgels. Nehalem countered with maiming fists and crippling boots, pulverizing flesh and fracturing bones, messing ugly guys even uglier... and giving Jessie time to climb swiftly the succession of short flights and slim triangular landings. But, she knew, he was not sacrificing his life to save her skin; he was savoring the brutal reflex of punishment to these men, while hoping, trusting, that she could save his skin later. This battle was lost, but as long as she was free to fight on, the war was not doomed.

Before she had crested the first landing, Jessie heard the furor of voices as a handful of men began rushing in pursuit.

"Did yuh eye the bastard what lammed up here?"

"Shit, he socked me in the eye! Slinky 'n tough, he was."

"Who can tell? Oughta have some lamps below to see by."

"Smallish fart, I rec'lect. Christ, watch it!"

"Shut up. It's darker on these steps than down there."

"He's gonna get smaller. I catch 'im, I'll cream 'im."

"Not here. Like the doc says, don't fluster the patients."

Jessie scurried higher as she felt the thin steps vibrating with the pummel of heavy feet. The few men had dodged by Nehalem, she surmised, not rolled over him, because she could hear from the ground floor the continuing melee, Nehalem still getting in a number of good licks while being overwhelmed.

The staircase ended on the second floor in a landing alcove off a main corridor. The sounds of chase were growing louder, nearer. And by the echoes reverberating along the hallway, Jessie could tell that others, in their attempt to capture Nehalem's accomplice, were approaching via the central staircase. But in one corner of the alcove, she glimpsed a thin wooden ladder that rose along one wall to a ceiling hatch. She clambered up its spindly rungs, assuming it led to the attic regions but not really caring, not really having any other choice.

Breathless, she reached the hatch and wrenched back the lock that held it closed. Without hesitating, she bent and crawled through the hatchway and onto a long slim gangplank that ran between the joists and ties of the roof. The hatch fell down into place, leaving her in a darkness that was unrelieved. So narrow was the passage that she could touch the rafters with either hand, and as far as she could judge, there was no room for even a mouse to hide.

She peered about anxiously, hearing the muffled trampling of searchers in the alcove below. Some yards to her left she spied another hatch—a roof vent that could be opened in case of inspections or repairs. It was just above the black bulk of a small cistern and was operated by a notched bar that hung downwards. Swiftly Jessie swung up on the cistern tank and thrust the iron arm upward. It refused to budge. Changing positions and teetering precariously on the tank's edge, she put both hands against the vent itself and shoved with all her might. Slowly, agonizingly so, the vent loosened from a frame warped with age and disuse, finally lifting just enough for a thin person to snake through.

Summoning her waning strength, Jessie hoisted herself up and onto the framework and eased out on a roof of pitch and laid with rust-red tiles. She turned, slid, moved to regain her footing, and slid again. Now she recalled why she hated tile roofs: Their slender, humped rows allowed precious little balance, and the tiles themselves clattered hollowly and sometimes cracked. These tiles were also treacherously slick, their porous clay having soaked in enough rain to float embedded oils and sediments to the surface, coating them with a glaze.

Very gingerly, she shifted into a crouch to close the vent. Her boots slipped out from under her, and stifling a startled yelp, Jessie groped frantically for the support of the vent frame. With one hand clutching the frame, she pressed the vent down. She almost had it shut flat when she stopped short, sucking in her breath.

The ceiling hatch below was creaking on dry hinges. She heard a man ask, "Where's this go?" and she forced herself to remain motionless, praying the tiles would do the same.

A panting voice, distantly heard, replied, "To the roof space, stupid. Where else? You gonna climb up in there?"

"Not if I can help it. Let the doc, if he wants."

"Yeah. Prob'ly enough rats there to chew your balls off."

The ceiling hatch thumped closed again. After a pause, Jessie let out her breath and tenderly finished lowering the vent in place. Then, distraught, she glanced about at the night. Moonlight dappled the slopes and silvered the rises and open spaces, and lanterns burned in a few cabins and tents. She knew by the glow cast from windows that lamps were lit in the offices and some other quarters of the main building, though her knowing caused her to wonder behind which window Nehalem was now. But darkness lay su-

99

preme and thick most everywhere.

The murk was almost a comforting shroud, masking her distress as she reflected upon the savaging Nehalem got. She doubted he'd confess who had set him loose. He may not be in any condition to talk now, but in any case, he was clinging to the faith in her doing it again. Successfully.

So obviously she couldn't stay here much longer. She'd be forced out by her obligations, if not by another, more thorough hunt—unless, that is, she wished to make her last stand here, clinging to the vent and single-handedly holding off the sanatorium with her pistol, derringer, and pockets of ammunition. Still, if push came to shove, she'd rather die that way and take her share of desperadoes with her. If she surrendered, or was caught alive, or was discovered to be Nehalem's rescuer, Augustas would do a little checking and quickly learn the cartel had posted open season on her—a sentence of death that would never be terminated until she was.

As a rescue, this attempt left quite a bit to be desired.

Chapter 11

Approaching the Nehalem ranch, Ki saw that the yard proper consisted of a large dairy barn, a milk house, a mess, a cookshack, and a bunkhouse, and several sheds, corrals, and holding pens grouped about a main house. The house itself was a square structure built of stone, save for its roof and eaves, with a gallery running around the place.

When they reined in by the house, Hope Nehalem said, "If you don't mind, Ki, I wish to break the news to my mother and sister."

Ki nodded, understanding her desire to be alone with them. "Of course. I'd like time to take care of my horse, anyway."

"Just tell Pops Shannon at the stable what you need."

Hope dismounted to go into the house, while Ki walked his weary pinto around the side, past the dairy barn, and to the stable. There were a few ranch hands working about, but nobody gave Ki more than a cursory glance, including the old geezer who sat propped on a stool against the front wall of the stable.

"You Shannon?" Ki asked them.

"Yep." The old-timer grinned. "You want something o' me?"

"I want my horse rubbed down and grained, if possible."

"Sure, I'll have 'er spiffied for you when you're ready to leave. You might be here a spell, if 'n you're looking for a job. Hafta see Norm Hodel, the foreman, and he's busy right now o'er the big house. You'll be wastin' your time, though, for there's some trouble visitin' hereabouts that don't make for kindly employment."

"So I gather," Ki replied dryly. "Thanks."

Pops Shannon opened his mouth as if he meant to warn Ki further, but Ki was already walking away. As he neared the house, Ki saw that Hope was now standing in a side doorway, nervously smoothing her palms down her flounced dress while talking to a man who faced her on the gallery. He was six feet three or four and had a great breadth of shoulder. His hair was black, he sported a large handlebar mustache, and he was twirling his Stetson in his hands as he conversed with the girl.

Ki paused for the discussion to end. Their voices raised slightly, and he heard the man say, "Maybe so, Hope, but Mr. Nehalem bein' missing ain't the reason you were ridin' north this morning."

"Was I riding, Norm?" Her voice was ascerbic. "Are you sure?"

"Chanced to see you myself, I did, just 'fore noon, headin' into them roughs by the fence line. And I saw somebody else comin' from the Box L. Wasn't quite close enough to see the jigger's face, but his build was mighty familiar, mighty durn familiar."

"I haven't the foggiest idea what you mean, Norman."

"Reckon you know full'n well," the man replied in significant tones. "Wouldn't Mr. Nehalem like to know who you was meetin'?"

Before the girl could respond, Ki stepped onto the gallery and intervened. "Hi, m'name's Ki, and I bet you must be the foreman, Norm Hodel," Ki rambled genially. "Couldn't help overhearing you spotting Miss Nehalem and myself getting together on account of her father. Sorry we missed seeing you, or we'd have returned all together."

Hodel gulped. "You? It was you I saw?" he demanded.

"Well, I'm from the Box L, and we met, didn't we, Hope?"

"We certainly did." The girl regarded Hodel, her lips firm. "I trust you're satisfied, Norm. Ki has volunteered to help find Dad, and he comes highly recommended as a tracker and hunter."

"From the Box L? That who recommended him? It's the same as the coyote recommending the fox to guard chickens." Hodel glanced from one to the other, his dark eyes narrowing and glittering. "I can help you more than he can, Hope, if you'd just listen up to me."

"I've listened before," the girl answered tiredly, "and I'm still not in the market for a husband. Right now I'm interested only in my father, Norm. You ought to be man enough to realize that."

Hodel fumbled with his hat, hesitated, and swallowed convulsively. "Well," he said at length, "reckon I'll be going back to my chores." He stalked from the gallery, his back stiff and his fingers twitching.

Ki turned to the girl. "I guess he did see Dwight, all right, but not close enough to be sure it was him. Luckily we're not that different in build, and Dwight's horse could be mistaken for my pinto at a distance. We didn't tell your foreman anything but the truth. Is he perhaps interested in you, too?"

"That's a rather personal question," she replied with a flirty smile. "But, yes, I suppose so. Trouble is, Norm can't tell me and my sister apart, never has been able to, and he's worked here fifteen years." She laughed. "I'm Faith, Ki. Hope's inside with Mother."

Ki chuckled. "You fooled me. You're the spitting image."

"Oh, we have our differences, if we care to show them." Her hand went back and forth over her lips as she met his gaze, then she opened the screen door, and turned with a languid swing to her hips, and Ki sensed some of those differences. Faith looked every bit as innocent as her sister Hope, as if she should be playing organ at some church, but it occurred to him that she could be the more dangerous of the twins—much more dangerous than any man around.

Trailing Faith inside, he entered a spacious parlor decorated with Indian rugs and bearskins. Hope was standing beside a wicker settee, and seeing her and Faith together, dresses and hair worn alike, Ki was struck even more by how identical they were. In the settee sat a stout, gray-haired woman wearing a gaily flowered wrapper that deepened the blue of her eyes. He bet her hair had once been blond.

"Very glad to meet you, Ki, and I thank you for your concern," Mrs. Nehalem said when they were introduced. She looked pale and anxious and, Ki was certain, fearful. "I knew, I felt, something had happened. You truly think you can locate Uriah?"

"I'll do my very best," Ki assured her. "We know your husband left town, so I believe checking along the trail is where to start."

"Before you go, please join us for a bite to eat."

Evidently nutrition was Mrs. Nehalem's contribution to solving trouble, Ki thought wryly, about to decline her invitation. Then he thought better of it and reluctantly agreed. He had much ground to cover before dark, but he was hungry and in need of the same short breather he was allowing his horse. The Nehalems were no less impatient, and they all were soon at table, enjoying a meal of cold chicken, fresh vegetables, bread, and coffee. Afterward, as Ki prepared to leave, he told them in low tones, "Don't worry. Everything will work out."

"I pray so," Mrs. Nehalem replied, and Hope nodded, a mist in her blue eyes. "If you say so, Ki, I'm sure it must be so."

Returning to the stable, Ki found no sign of Pops Shannon, though some ranch hands were around, apparently having returned from a shift out on the range. There was none of the indifference previously given him; now tension and hostility were almost palpable, and Ki had the impression they were grouped by the stable waiting for him. Norm Hodel was among them, and he walked out to meet Ki. It didn't take much to figure what the prod was over—Hodel had been popping his mouth off and was planning to prove his words by bracing Ki.

"Ain't no skirts here'n now, boy. What's your true game?"

Ki eyed the foreman, who had no discernible expression on his face, and he realized that being pleasant about this would gain him nothing. "You were told once, boy, and that should be sufficient. Uppity Chink, too." Hodel stepped closer, scowling now. "It seems mighty peculiar to me, mighty durn peculiar, that we know this spread top to bottom, but we don't find hide nor hair of the boss, an' we ain't asked to look, neither. Not us, no, while you just ride in from the Box L and convince the ladies you're positive you can bring him right home. How come?"

The foreman's tone indicated his suspicions that Ki himself was responsible for Nehalem's disappearance and naturally would know where to locate him. "Maybe I just want to find him more than you do," Ki retorted, cold and clipped.

Hodel stiffened, resentment and distrust glowing in his eyes, and Ki thought, here it comes. Ki did not know how the girl got there, or which one of the twins she was, for he had been so intent on watching Hodel and his crew that everything else had become extraneous. He was setting himself for the expected attack, already deciding not to use his lethal martial arts, which would look too strange and exotic to the crew and only add to their hostility. Besides, he was irritated enough by Hodel's jealous antagonism to relish the idea of beating the man at his own brawling sport. So Ki was setting himself to respond accordingly when abruptly the Nehalem girl was there, panting hard and halting just aside of them.

"Norman Hodel, who do you think you are," she snapped angrily, "to stand there making a fist at Ki when you should shake his hand?"

"Step away," Hodel snarled, glaring at Ki. "Step away."

"I won't step away. You started this; you stop it."

"Step away," he repeated, hard and unyielding. "Nobody can call me out like he did and get away with it." And he suddenly charged, wading in and swinging measured blows at Ki.

Ki ducked and weaved aside, knowing he should just keep on moving before matters worsened and aware that goading Hodel had been foolish. Yet something defiant was stirring in his mind, and he cut in swiftly to land a short, vicious, and well-controlled punch to his belly. All it did was made the big man grunt and rush to close, eyes gleaming with anticipation. Again Ki danced away, appraising his opponent, assessing his strengths and weaknesses.

Hodel outweighed him by a good thirty pounds. The power of the foreman was obviously tremendous, his body too heavily muscled to be harmed. One solid connection with his fist would put Ki permanently out of the fight. Only strong, repeated punches to the jaw might have any effect, Ki thought. He dipped under one of Hodel's roundhouse swings and landed his fist on the side of Hodel's jaw with a sharp and plainly audible crack. This time Hodel staggered back, a look of pure surprise on his enraged face. Ki followed and snapped a second blow to Hodel's jaw before the foreman could recover.

Ki retreated quickly as Hodel lunged toward him again. The man's face was red from exertion and shiny with sweat, his breath coming in short, gusty pants. His eyes were slightly glazed. Ki grinned tauntingly, now knowing Hodel had another weakness—he was short of breath, as well as having a glass jaw. He shifted and feinted, evading Hodel's storming fists, stabbing two lefts to Hodel's chin so fast that they appeared to be one echoing punch.

Then a brutal knuckler cracked alongside Ki's cheek, momentarily stunning him. Hodel wrapped a strangling arm around his neck and was about to bash his face in with stiff finishers, when Ki butted back, hard, smacking Hodel in the nose. Breaking free, he launched another one-two combination as Hodel stumbled backward, blood gushing from his nostrils. His left caught Hodel in the nose again, flattening its bridge, while his right punched him square in the eye. Like a blundering, half-blind bear, Hodel tried to slug in return, but Ki dived under the wild swings and pummeled him on the chin, driving Hodel back more. Dazed and bloodied, Hodel began to sag, his crew muttering threats but held at bay by the girl.

Ki carefully gauged his next punch. A blistering uppercut, it hit Hodel on his battered chin, and Hodel arched backward and sat down hard, dust showering up around him. Then he fell limp.

Ki stood above the stilled figure for a moment, his chest heaving. Hodel's eyes flickered slightly and Ki walked away, through the mumbling crew and into the stable. His pinto mare was ready, and Ki led her out, ignoring the crew but keeping a cautious watch on Hodel, who had regained his feet and was brushing himself off.

With a thin grin, Ki asked, "You got more complaints?"

Hodel did not speak immediately, but glared at Ki as though running something through his mind. Finally he said, "I don't like you, mister. I don't like your ways." He paused and sucked in a ragged breath, glancing at the girl and then back at Ki. "I've got my eye on you, and the first funny move you make, I'll cut you down."

"Anytime, boy, anytime," Ki replied through his teeth,

swinging up into the saddle. He nodded at the girl. "Sorry, Miss Nehalem."

"Don't be, Ki. Norm reaped what he sowed; that's a rarity."

"I'll be seeing you shortly. And, again, don't do any worrying. Everything will work out all right, I'm sure."

He rode away at a leisurely pace, tired but refusing to show it, worried but refusing to admit it. The crew huddled around the foreman.

Once out of sight of the ranch, Ki sent the pinto loping along the trail that connected the ranch with the town. It unraveled eastward through the same kind of open country that characterized the range he'd crossed earlier when getting to the ranch. Scattered bunches of dairy cattle grazed idly, while ahead and to the north lay a ridge of low hills, like a barrier between Nehalem's land and yonder regions of Rainbow Valley.

He scouted for Nehalem, hoping the cowman would show up as the victim of an accident rather than foul play. Doubting that, however, he mainly concentrated on off-trail signs, realizing there wasn't much point in studying traces of ordinary travel on the oft-used course. On occasion he would halt for closer inspection of the shoulders and fringes, but otherwise he kept to his chore with some steadiness, not hurrying but moving as rapidly as care would permit. It was pretty discouraging, the storm having blotted out whatever marks might have been made before its arrival.

Late afternoon found Ki about three-quarters of the way to Elbow. The hills now paralleled him on his left, and the trail was curving down between the boulders and scrub of an arroyo. It was a short patch, the trail continuing on up and into a straightaway that would eventually, Ki figured, connect with the town road that went south across Sangrar Wash. Right here, though, was a natural spot for ambush, certainly the best he'd come upon so far. Feeling it worth a look, Ki cut from the trail and dipped along the arroyo.

He spotted nothing of interest on the southern edge of the trail, so he doubled back and prowled up the other side. The storm's runoff had gouged channels in the arroyo's bottom, but higher on its eastern bank, where bush willow and arrow grass screened the trail, Ki saw where four horses had stood for some while. Hooftracks and bootprints were scarce, but Ki scrutinized what there were, along with the many washed droppings and soggy cigarette butts that littered the ground. It took him a length of time, but Ki managed to detect where the riders, having waited at this point, had barged through the undergrowth to the trail and then returned with a fifth horseman.

Ki was staring northward, estimating where the five riders then had gone, when suddenly his pinto perked its head and whinnied. An answering neigh came from behind him. His initial instinct was to duck, but then he glimpsed the rider trotting from the direction of the ranch, and he turned his horse back to the trail, annoyed.

The girl was wearing a bonnet that matched her dress; the braids of her blond hair swung free and flashed like gold in the sunset. She pulled up her dun in front of Ki and eyed him from under long lashes that veiled, but did not hide, the challenge in her glance. Her voice was throaty. "I hoped I'd catch you."

"Not hope," Ki said. "It took Faith to come after me."

She smiled, her tongue touching her lips. "You positive?"

"Like you said, Faith, there're differences in character if not in appearance. Has something happened, or are you just meddling?"

"Meddling!" she snapped, losing her smile. "No, nothing in particular is worse off than when you left. But this spread is more mine than it is yours, Ki, and no Nehalem sends strangers to do a dangerous job a Nehalem should do!"

"There's no danger. It's still no place for you."

"Maybe, maybe not, but I'm here. What've you learned?"

Ki shrugged, knowing it would be useless to argue further. "Just before the storm, right about the time your father would've passed by, four riders came out of the arroyo. Five went back in." He led her into the arroyo and showed her the evidence. "One rider's a heavy smoker. One horse—there, you see?—has a habit of sliding its right rear hoof when turning. They headed up this arroyo, but last night's rain pretty well scrubbed their sign."

"They kidnapped Dad, no question." She shuddered for a moment; then the trembling left her and she was calm again, gazing beyond the arroyo at the distant ridges. "Stands to reason they crossed the flats in a direct push, fast as possible, for those hills somewhere."

Ki nodded. "Yeah, through that low notch there in the hill chain would be my guess. It's the only natural passage around."

"Let's go find out." Faith spurred her dun up the arroyo.

Ki struck after her, muttering. "She's too old to spank and too young to have sense—the perfect age for trouble."

Chapter 12

Soon Ki and Faith reached a caved-in chunk along the eastern bank of the arroyo. Despite the storm, there were clear indications that this short landslide had been used to climb up onto ground level.

They followed, and as evening descended around them, they angled out across the rolling grassland for the notched hillside. It was not easy, but every so often Ki picked up a hoofprint, cigarette stub, or similar clue that proved they were on the right track. At first these infrequent traces led them only slightly more deeply into the rough country, but soon they began rising on a twisty course through erosive culverts and between massive boulders, a route that would conceal riders from view.

Faith voiced Ki's thought, "Any riders who'd go to so much trouble to climb a nasty slope must have a nasty reason for it."

She rode alongside Ki now, and with seeming inadvertence, her dun kept dancing sideways, bumping foreshoulders with his pinto. Ki also grew aware that her knee liked to nudge his thigh, and that she rode closer than was absolutely necessary, swaying toward him and faintly smiling in her tantalizing manner.

Darkness beat them to the notched draw through the hills. The ascent steepened and grew more rugged, and from a ledge about midway to the notch, they saw that the sun had sunken and only a brassy afterglow remained behind a shimmering horizon. Their path ahead was lost in the blue heat of dusk. Ki tried nonetheless, dismounting by some nearby growth to search for anything that might lead them on.

Faith sat slim and straight in her saddle, watching him, her eyes shadowed and unreadable. Her dun ambled over and nuzzled his pinto. Then both horses put their heads down and began to graze.

Ki shook his head as he reviewed the swiftly blackening area. "This is as far as we can go."

"A shame. I'd have liked to go all the way with you."

They did not speak for a minute, just stared at each other. Ki could not judge her comment by the expression of her shaded eyes, but he was very aware of the pattern of her breasts under her bodice and the snug fit of the dress over her hips. Faith broke their stare. She swung a leg lithely over her saddle cantle and stepped down.

"What do you think of me, Ki?"

"What do you mean?"

"I know you think I'm easy. You think I'm wanton."

"That's not true."

She was now so close he could feel her warm breath and smell her rose-scented soap. Her chin was raised and her uptilted face was yearning. "What else can you think of me, acting this way?"

"That you're restless and bored."

"Well, it is dull living here." She pouted. "Did you know that we're actually triplets? We are, and sister Charity is already married and has a fat baby and is bored silly. Oh, I've had my chances, and Norman is nice in his way, but the boys around here are such louts. Even Dwight Latimer, though he and Hope will get hitched before long."

"Then it really will get dull," Ki said, growing aroused but also growing leery of playing her game. "Your father can rant and rave all he wants about the Latimers and sheepmen in general—until the day comes they're his in-laws. And becoming a grandfather has a way of changing a fair number of feuding notions, too."

"Believe me, I'm looking forward to boredom from that." She placed a hand on his arm. "But not now. Don't you bore me, Ki."

Reaching out, Ki grabbed her by the arms. He was impulsive and rough as he pulled her toward him, bruising his mouth down on hers. He could feel her tense and begin to resist. Good, he told himself, she will break away and that would be the end of her teasing.

In the midst of this conviction, Ki felt fire come into her mouth. Her arms went around him and amazed him with the strength and fierceness of their embrace. Her hand rose and the nails dug into the back of his neck. And when finally she took her lips from his, she did not pull away but pressed warm and firm against him, her head thrown back a little, her mouth parted, and her blue eyes burning.

"Now that," she whispered huskily, "is more like it."

Ki untied her bonnet and drew it off. Breathing audibly, she plucked it from him and tossed it down, then began unfastening her dress, bunching it loosely, and shrugging it up over her head. Ki followed suit, quickly shucking off his vest and shirt and dropping them on the growing pile of clothes while she discarded her stockings and chemise, baring her nubile, raspberry-tipped breasts. Then on tiptoes, she brought her mouth to his; their mouths barely touched, lips tingling at the promised contact, cherishing the promise before the act. Ki embraced her, his hands on her hips and gliding along the silken stretch of her pantaloons, waiting for her to act first.

Faith did. Deftly she undid the knot of his rope belt and popped the buttons of his fly, tugging his jeans down, slowly, her hands inching over his thighs to free his burgeoning erection. Now Ki moved to do the same to the string of her pantaloons, opening them and lowering them

113

just to the very point where the cleft between her legs began to show. He leaned back deliberately and saw that her hair was almost as blond there—a delicate sweep growing along her mound, just a puff. She stroked his rigid shaft lightly, rubbing its blunt crown . . . then together they finished undressing each other, stepping aside for a moment to stand naked, eyeing themselves, before slipping down on the mattress of their garments.

His fingers slid gently up the inside of her legs. He stroked her loins, while he bent and kissed each nipple, her shoulders, the smooth line of her throat, and each fluttering eyelash. Even when Faith writhed against his caresses, begging him, he still worked her slowly, lightly, feeling the volcano of passion boiling inside her and crying for release. Then, moaning with deep animal purrings, Faith pushed him on his back to receive her erotic fondlings. She shifted to kiss him again and give him her tongue, sighing with pleasure.

Ki felt her tremble, felt her weight, and enjoyed her ardent advances as she kissed his neck and ears and his tiny nipples. Her mouth laved fire on his chest, then teased lower, moving past the navel and dipping to his inner thighs. And when the tension was unbearable, she went down on his prod, trying to swallow all of his girth. Ki stiffened, tensing his muscles. She dug her hands under his hips and encouraged his motions, taking as much as she could. Her tongue was rough, taunting his sensitivity. Then she took the length of him and slid back again his entire length to repeat, and repeat again, her lips clasping him in a tight oval.

"You . . . you better be ready," Ki panted in warning.

Faith laughed. She climbed on top of Ki, undulating as she lowered herself, slowly enveloping his rigid shaft until she squatted, pressing against him. Ki gasped as she impaled herself and was reminded of how her twin sister had

114

looked riding Glenn Latimer. She hovered above him, thrusting with her hip and buttock muscles, pumping his hardness as fast as she could, pummeling Ki against their clothes wadded beneath him. Ki responded with a quickening tempo of pistoning surges to match her frenzied rhythm, sucking one swaying breast into his mouth, flicking her distended nipple with his tongue, and grasping her other breast with his hand.

Her desire continued building to an insane pitch. She writhed and squirmed in a dozen different wriggling directions. Ki felt his excitement mounting higher and sensed he was on the brink of release. The tang of her sweat was on his tongue; her dilated gaze glowed with ecstasy as, together, they hammered at yet a faster pace, pushing deeper, their naked bodies slapping and rubbing tempestuously.

Faith tried to say something, but she could no longer speak. She mewled, shivering from the electric impact of her orgasm while the hot jets of Ki's bursting climax flooded deep inside her belly. He pulled her tighter to his pulsing groin as they seemingly merged flesh and bone. Then he collapsed, exhausted and drained. Faith fell across him, stretching her legs back so she could lie with him clamped inside her, their bodies entwined.

Finally, almost drowsily, she said, "Uh-uh," and reluctantly slid off him. "I have to piddle," she explained demurely, and she flitted off behind one of the boulders.

Ki just lay there in a stupor. Then abruptly there came to his ears another sound, farther away in the direction of the notch—a faint clicking noise like that made by the beat of horses' irons on stony ground.

Scrambling up, he padded naked to the end of the ledge and glanced up at the dark bulk of the hills. The night did not seem quite so black now, moonglow and starlight enabling him to scan the outlines of the rocky terrain. For a long moment there were no more betraying sounds, but when they came—the slight jingling of metal against metal—he felt sure they came from that suspected passage.

He squatted motionless, peering up at the dark hillsides. The beat of irons grew louder. Topping a distant ridge that swelled upward from a deep hollow, he perceived a group of horsemen. One by one they appeared, as if drawn by invisible strings, and there they stood clearly against the murky night sky. Ki counted eight before they turned and followed the crest of the ridge, which ran westward with a slight veering to the south.

Faith came to him, shamelessly nude, her eyes dreamy and half-closed, her flesh still hot to the touch. She hunkered beside him, curling against his shoulder.

"Shh," he cautioned and pointed at the riders.

She pressed tighter, catching sight of the mysterious group. There was something furtive and purposeful about those slow-moving horsemen. After another minute, they pulled to a halt and seemed to be staring westward down the slope as they bunched together. Then single file they vanished as strangely as they had appeared.

"What're they up to?" Faith asked in a hushed voice.

"Up to no good," Ki replied softly. "Late-working ranch hands don't head home by skulking among the rocks."

"I agree. Let's trail them."

Returning to their well-flattened pile of clothes, they swiftly sorted garments and dressed and then checked rigging, tightened cinches, and mounted. As an afterthought, Faith dug into one of her pouches and brought out a .38 Remington revolver, which for quick convenience she tucked in the bunched lap of her skirt.

They jigged their horses toward the hogback where they'd spied the riders. It was a hard scramble up the broken ground, and once there, they paused to get their bearings before angling westward and following the backhill trail by the echoing sounds of passage. They tried to keep

116

their own noise to an absolute minimum. For a long time the riders remained invisible, lost in the night and distance ahead as they traveled the hollows and ridges, skirted some banks, and curved among a series of gaps and tables. Eventually the stretch of hills began petering out. Ki and Faith negotiated a steep slope and were just poking their heads over the crest when Ki motioned to veer slightly so that they topped the slope where a bristle of growth cast a deep gloom across the exposed summit.

The other side was jagged, rubbled terrain where only renegades and predators would care to tread. Almost at the bottom, the eight riders were descending from a slender bench along a route that twisted among scrub and stone to a small notch in the floor of the valley. From there on was rolling pasture, mile upon mile of it with hardy grass and tufted thickets and clumps of bedded cattle. Yonder was the Nehalem ranch, its buildings swallowed by night, only the tower of its windmill visible like a landmark.

"Looks like maybe they're aiming for our place," Faith said fretfully and touched her revolver. "Shall I shoot to head them off?"

Ki shrugged. "At a thousand yards, you'll just warn them."

"Yes, and they may hit back at us with rifles. I don't care for those odds." She started her dun down the slope, adding grimly, "Even if they did scatter, they'd only regroup and come again some other night. And we still don't know what they're after, either."

Well before they reached level ground, they could hear the riders galloping toward the ranch. Once clear of the bottom notch, they lashed their horses in fast pursuit, favoring the brush and pools of shadows so they would not be spotted by any of the distant horsemen who might glance back behind. Gradually the black silhouette of the ranch buildings took shape, their roofs etched in moonglow, Chaparral growth and a straggling grove covered the slight rise of a low, flat hillock on which the ranch was situated. All was quiet, the Nehalems and their crew soundly asleep, it now being somewhere between midnight and one, as best Ki could judge. The suspicious riders were no longer seen or heard at all.

Ki felt anxious. "Faith, I think perhaps you should've shot."

She shook her head. "This way, if they're at the ranch readying to raise hell, we'll stop them in the act. But what *is* their act?"

Abruptly they had a startling answer to her question. They were approaching the ranch on a tangent, and the most prominent feature facing them was the end of the big dairy barn, its blank wall broken only by a window. As they rode toward it, that window suddenly began to twinkle, as if a weakly flickering candle were held against it. But the feeble light strengthened and spread—within seconds flaring to an ominous carmine glow, the sound of crackling flames becoming audible even at the considerable distance.

"They've fired the barn!" she cried. "Hurry!"

They urged their horses to greater speed, tearing across the remaining expanse of grassland and charging up the small rise to the ranch yard. Branches whipped their faces and thorns ripped at their clothes and raked their horses' flanks, but they plunged heedlessly on up the rock-strewn slope with undiminished haste. Faith hefted her revolver in preparation for firing an alarm and arousing the crew. Then came a shocked yell from the bunkhouse, and guns began roaring all about the place, streaking the night with savage blasts. Lead shattered windows and drummed into wood as the eight riders drove the awakened defenders back inside the bunkhouse.

Flames had crept up the corners of the barn and now they caught on to the eaves and roof shingles. Boards crackled and popped in imitation of the gunshots that were ringing out through the yard. Bullets poured to and from the main house as well as the bunkhouse. One of the attackers was barking orders to move out in a throaty voice that Ki instantly recognized as being that of Froggy Tode. An agonized scream came then, and Ki hoped it was Tode who'd been hit. But Tode called again to move out.

He and Faith were perhaps four hundred yards from the barn and racing toward a final straggle of growth when, out of the last bank of chaparral, crashed the band that now had seven riders. There was no time to wheel, to turn aside. Straight at the tight group they headed, seeing the glint of raised guns and hearing the shouts of surprise. Faith leveled her revolver and started triggering, while Ki began flicking *shuriken* in a fanning crescent before them. A rider howled and went hurtling from his saddle. Another gasped retchingly twice and pitched forward before sliding groundward.

The flames of the burning barn soared, a reddish, unholy glare illuminating the ranch yard and slope. Into the milling group Ki and Faith surged with no sense of fear, only a fierce, evil joy. Guns blazed. The air quivered to the roar of the reports. Ki felt the breath of lead against his face as he searched vainly for Tode. He did see another rider reel in his saddle, clutching the horn for support, a *shuriken* protruding from his breastbone. And he saw Faith flailing right and left with her empty revolver, as her dun barged against a horse and hurled it off its feet. He felt something liquid spurting over his hand as a man cried out in great pain, and then, finally, he glimpsed Froggy Tode at the fringe of the action.

Ki reined his pinto, but he was too hemmed in to turn much, so he twisted hard about in the saddle to get a line on Tode. The impulse to kill was strong—only the innocent died in this war, it seemed; the ones who merited death continued to live so they might plunder and murder more. Before he could snap a *shuriken* or two at Tode, a salvo of slugs screeched between them, so close that it caused Ki to duck and his horse to shy askew, upsetting his aim. Tode glanced at the barrage, eyed Ki, and lunged away, his bulging orbs glowering with fury. By then Ki and Faith were through the tangle of maddened horses and shooting men, their furious momentum sending them on into the thicket, while the surviving attackers beat a frantic retreat down across the flats toward the distant hills.

Reaching the upper fringe of the growth, they did not pause to view the fleeing riders, but goaded their horses directly toward the barn. Its entire roof was now spouting flame and smoke, and from inside came lowing and bawling of such witless terror that it turned the nape of Ki's neck to ice. Lights were being lit in the ranch house and bunk house, and as Ki and Faith stormed up, half-clad men poured into the yard—babbling, dazed, and confused.

"Blankets!" Ki shouted, leaving his saddle at a run. "Grab your blankets; bring them fast! We have to get the cattle out!"

The crewmen tumbled back into the bunkhouse and reappeared with their arms full of stripped bed clothing. Ki seized a blanket and led the assault on the barn, inside of which was a bedlam of panic. The blaze was latching onto the ceiling boards with a gushing rush of sound, sparks sifting through and smoke billowing. The heat seemed to sizzle the sweat beading the men's scared faces.

In the nearest stall was a kicking longhorn stud. It was dehorned and haltered to the manger. There was no time to unbuckle the straps. Ki unsheathed his short, curve-bladed *tanto* and cut. The freed bull promptly hoofed him in the ribs. He gasped with the pain and shock, but fought the terrified animal as it punched out a whole side of the manger. He wrapped the blanket around its head and choused it from the barn. After him came the ranch hands, battling other fear-crazed but more manageable Holsteins and Guernseys to safety.

"Don't let your cows run back in," Ki shouted at Pops Shannon, who came lumbering up, his old-fashioned nightshirt flapping about his bare legs. "Except maybe for that damnable longhorn!"

"Wal, don't you go in there again, neither!" Shannon bellowed, as Ki turned back. "The floor's saggin'! You'll get caught!"

Ignoring the warning, Ki darted into the burning barn. A main timber gave way and dropped in a shower of sparks, its blast of heat striking Ki with an almost physical impact and searing the air he drew into his lungs as he wrestled a smaller, reddish-brown cow to the door. Just as he reached it, the ceiling crumbled with a deafening crash. Instantly the barn interior was a mass of consuming flame, the doorway a fiery ring collapsing in on itself.

Hurrawing the hysterical cow, Ki forced it through the blazing door and leaped out right after it, scorched and singed but not seriously hurt. Then, wiping the sweat and ashes from his face, he went to a nearby water trough and dunked himself.

Across the yard, some of the crew were corraling the rescued cattle, while others were containing the fire, so it wouldn't jump to adjacent structures as the barn burned itself to cinders. By the ranch house porch stood Mrs. Nehalem, daughters Hope and Faith, and Norm Hodel. The foreman signaled for Ki to come join them.

Mrs. Nehalem held herself courageously firm. "We're extremely grateful to you, Ki. I'm not sure I fully understand what this is all about, though Faith has explained how you trailed those fiends after chancing on them while tracking my husband. Is there anything more you can or wish to add?"

There were a few details he did not dare to add and which he doubted Faith had volunteered. "Not really," he replied, shaking his head. "I'm glad to've gotten here to help, but I'm sorry it was because I failed to locate Uriah

before dark. Oh—this was not the work of the Box L."
Tersely Ki spoke of recognizing Froggy Tode.

"Now maybe you'll believe me that the Latimers aren't
monsters," Hope told her mother and the foreman, and she
sighed relief as she faced Ki. "Yes, thank you, and when
you find Dad, and I know you will, he'll thank you, too.
That last cow you risked your life to bring out is our only
Jersey."

"Hush, child, Ki isn't interested in your father's cows,"
Mrs. Nehalem said to Hope and then regarded Faith with
an expression implying she suspected what might have occurred. "Faith, you have your clothes on, so you can take
Ki back and show him where he can wash the soot off
properly," she instructed, and indeed, she and Hope had
little on save their dressing gowns. "He can sleep in the
spare room off the parlor. If you'll all excuse us, I think
it's time Hope and I retired. Good night."

Mother and daughter went up the steps and into the
house. Faith waited until the door shut and then murmured
to Ki, "I didn't say one word wrong, didn't even look
wrong. I swear Mom's a mind reader."

"Uh, before you go," Hodel declared, as Ki started to
leave with Faith. "Mrs. Nehalem speaks for us, Ki, for the
whole crew. The stud bull you pulled out first is a special
longhorn and is kinda our mascot, Mist' Nehalem's pet
favorite."

By now Pops Shannon and a half dozen other hands
were clustered around and growled agreement. Their eyes
were hard, their lids set in straight lines, but they offered
little comment. That was their foreman's duty, and Hodel
finished his apology. "Mighty shameful, mighty durn
shameful how we—and me the worstest—treated you, Ki.
Wouldn't blame you none to tell us all to go to hell."

"I've a thick hide." Ki grinned, extending his hand.
"Norm, you're a big man, a smart man. You're a man to
stick with."

Hodel pumped hands vigorously, pleased by Ki's high compliment. "Y'know, what with Mist' Nehalem gettin' stole and this wokenin' up to shootin' and torchin', we'd be bound to Box L settle scores if not for you. But we'll bite the fuse awhile, seein' as you swear it was Froggy Tode and not the Latimers behind this tonight. Though danged if I can reckon why a town gambler would want to raid us."

"You answered yourself. It's to prod you into striking the Box L; last night, the Box L was hit and figured you did it."

"T'hell we did! Them muttonheads better not blame us!"

Faith laughed a shade scornfully. "If they still did, they'd have been here long before this. But they wised up, so now you wise up. Both spreads are being framed into feuding. Right, Ki?"

Ki nodded. "More exactly, an old personal row is being kindled into open war between you and the Box L. No, I don't know why, nor if Tode is working alone or for someone else, but . . ." He paused to gaze at the barn. His grin became thin, his voice growing soft as buckskin. "But I won't wait to trace Tode and his gang back to their rathole and catch them in the trap they've been snaring us in. I can't wait—because they don't wait."

"Wal, wait a bit longer," a ranch hand called, trotting up. "Somebody's coming 'long the trail as if riding for his life!"

Chapter 13

Up the stairs from the fight, up the ladder, along the crawl space, and up to the roof. Maybe five minutes, Jessie estimated as she gripped the vent; from then to now, she spent five minutes to cap a failure she wasted a whole afternoon to plan mistakenly.

Well, she couldn't rectify it by hiding here.

And now was as good a time as any, she supposed, to go try doing it right. She hadn't heard a sound in the attic beneath her since those two men had peeked through the ceiling hatch. Better yet, the hunt evidently was focusing outside, she gathered by listening to thrashings of brush that echoed up from the grounds and by seeing men searching in much the way beaters would seek to corner prey.

The vent proved almost as stubborn as before. This time she had to haggle with it while grappling for traction on the slick tiles, but gradually she pried the flap open. She didn't bother to pause and listen, figuring her struggles would have tipped anyone in the crawl space—but she did suddenly hesitate, swiveling to peer down over the roof's edge, drawn by a riotous eruption at the main entrance below. Then she froze, astounded.

Uriah Nehalem burst into view, draped in men. He tore them off and they tore back on, and for each one he flung aside, another leeched a hold, trying to drag him down while he stumbled and blundered in his convulsive rampage to escape. Their yelling, cursing, scuffling pandemonium touched off the other men who'd been beating the bushes, and they came sprinting to add their weight. Still resisting, Nehalem was slowed to a floundering halt by the anchor of bodies.

Jessie watched the ringing men pounce for the kill. Nehalem parried a punch with an uppercut and slammed a knee into another attacker's groin, while chopping the side of his hand across someone else's face, cracking bones. Two men tackling him were snagged, one by each of his sledgehammer fists and then their heads were bashed together. Before they had fallen, he was mauling yet another man, fighting to break out, an experienced tavern brawler who refused to be taken easily. By comparison, Jessie thought, this made his bout with Glenn Latimer seem like a tussle between girls in pinafores.

But the men finally engulfed Nehalem. Sweaty, dusty, angry at having to exert themselves, they surged, arms seizing and clubs smashing. Nehalem stumbled and was pulled to the ground just as Doc Augustas stepped from the front door, wringing his hands, and stood on the porch to call plaintively, "The poor bloke is crazed! Don't harm him more than necessary!"

Callous blarney for public consumption, Jessie thought contemptuously and saw it was being soundly ignored by the men. Yet Nehalem battered his way to his feet again using hands, elbows, knees, his entire body as a weapon. But it was hopeless. He got clobbered in a vise of three attendants, six sets of knuckles landing simultaneously, and he hit the dirt again, snuffed like a candle.

Some of the men carried Nehalem into the main house with Doc Augustas, some returned to the hunt, and some merely drifted off. The flurry had attracted few spectators, probably due to many patients being comatose from Augustas' medicines, and others shying away. Those who had ventured out turned back, discussing the unfortunate one's case among themselves.

A peace of sorts quickly descended. Again, for a moment, Jessie scanned the darkness, admiring the spray of stars and the glow of moon toying with the shadows. It was sufficiently brilliant to bathe the grounds, and Jessie, from her vantage point, readily spotted a buggy stopping at the main gate. It was a common two-seater, and though she could not see the driver, she wasn't much concerned about it. She had more urgent matters.

She squeezed through the vent and crouched on the cistern. Then crawling down onto the gangplank, she went very slowly back to the ceiling hatch, which she eased up just enough to be able to check below. Finding the alcove empty and hearing no sounds from the hallway, she opened the hatch a bit more and slid through, dangling for a moment before her feet caught the top rung of the ladder. Climbing down, she tiptoed cautiously to the rear staircase and descended to the ground floor, where she peered carefully in both directions before dipping silently through the serving pantry and dining room to the corridor and then along to the foyer. She was just starting across the foyer toward the corridor to Wing B when the front door unlatched. She pivoted quickly as it swung open.

She found herself face to face with Quentin Pollard.

It was difficult to say who looked more startled. Recovering, Jessie flashed the spriteliest smile she could muster and blathered, "I do declare, Mr. Pollard, what a pleasant surprise. I thought that I saw your buggy pull up just now. Doc Augustas swears I'm in a frightful condition but figures he may be able to save me for a few more years. Or was it after a few years? Well, ne'er mind. I simply had to come thank you for your note. It's led to a world of cure."

"Pleased to've been of service." Pollard had shut the door and was waddling down the foyer, Jessie falling in alongside. "You mind his prescriptions, m'dear."

"Oh, Quentin!" Augustas, who had emerged from the office, sang out sharply. "Will you come in here at once?"

"On my way. All right, Miss Starbuck, I'll see you anon." Pollard smiled and hastened to go inside with Augustas.

Soon as the office door closed, Jessie veered into the rear connecting corridor that ran beside Augustas' examination room. She was especially quiet when passing abreast of it, fearing her footfalls might be audible. She heard a low murmuring of voices through the wall and wondered how she should try to overhear Augustas and Pollard. Adjacent to the room she glimpsed a door which, she was swift to discover, was to a large linen closet. She eased inside and gently latched the door behind her, hoping she would be able to listen to their conversation through its wall.

There was a total absence of light and a heavy reek of bleach and naptha, but she felt her way along until she reached a point where the muted talk seemed loudest. Crouching, she quietly moved piles of sheets and pillowcases aside, and then with ears straining, she leaned forward to catch what fragments of voice might filter through. To her delight, she found she could not only hear, but see as well. Evidently, she surmised, the closet had originally been part of the room, and the remodeling had been done rather poorly, for there was a thin crack between the room's wainscot and the paneling of the upper wall, which had gone unnoticed due to the linen stacked against it. Thanking heaven for this amazing stroke of luck, Jessie squinted through the slit, spying on the two men in the room.

"I sent for Muldow, and after he's here and dealt with, you can go," Augustas was saying, pacing moodily with his hands clasped behind him. "Nothing in your line can help the Nehalem situation."

"Can't admit I'm sorry." Pollard was seated, pouring a drink of his favorite medicine. "Sounds like Uriah turned maniacal. D'you think perhaps that Starbuck woman had a hand in letting him loose?"

"Very droll. A flighty female hypochondriac frees her local enemy and bests my men. Ha. Ha," Augustas replied, not laughing. "Nehalem won't tell, and the only solid eyewitness, the wing's guard, died of a concussion. We've searched cellar to roof and now we're patrolling the grounds, but I suspect whoever it was has fled the area."

"Likely so, Doc. All I know is, ever since Abram Volner came and chanced to recognize you, there seems to be a Starbuck finger of some sort and to some degree in everything that's gone sour for us.

"Starbuck was a foul trick perpetrated by Thad Latimer, so naturally they'd now be involved. It doesn't matter. I've three of Tode's boys set to remove Nehalem soon's they've finished visiting our soiled doves—y'know, the girls we got for the rogues whom our investors insist on sending here on get-away-from-the-law vacations. No harm done, and it's like a bonus for dispatching Nehalem promptly on cue."

"I see. Is Froggy hiding here, too?"

"No, he's with his gang up in the hills, but we've kept in touch and worked this out." Augustas sighed. "If I'd foreseen Nehalem's disruption, I might've changed our plan and dispensed with him last night. Still, a day-old corpse just won't pass examination as a fresh one, so on balance, it's wiser to've waited till tonight."

"Wiser I don't see. Keeping him alive doesn't make sense."

"It doesn't have to make sense. It has to make trouble, and that it shall. Last night, while Tode was indisposed, I had Delahaney ramrod a strike against the Box L. So tonight, after Tode hits Nehalem's spread and Nehalem is later found shot, it'll appear as if the Box L killed him during a retaliatory raid."

"Or Froggy will be rumored to've done it," Pollard countered, pouring another drink. "He's a jailbreaking robber, after all, who was dumb enough to've got caught in the act. And you had to go to a lot of fuss to rescue him or he'd have turned on us. Face it, the man's been reckless and untrustworthy, and now he's a liability."

"I'm doing my job, Quentin, and you're doing okay publicizing the sanatorium and handling legal affairs, but sometimes violence is the only way to solve a problem—such as the Starbuck courier. We'd be in a pretty mess without Tode, and we owe him reciprocal aid. Moreover, he's the vital link with our investors. He heard they were looking for methods to rig a vast, posh, safe hide-out and remembered me."

"Ah, yes, our glorious benefactors," Pollard replied, liquor making him sarcastic and argumentative. "They flog us to produce the entire valley for 'em overnight. We take all the risks doing it, while they hide in the East behind accents too thick to cut."

"So what if they're German tycoons? Half my patients can't speak decent English, either. You'd prefer to go back to the way it was? To the futility of insignificant law cases that didn't pay, to ranchers who've no use for legalities, to washing your own linen? I don't. Neither does Tode. We don't ever again want to shill medicine shows, secretly brew tapeworm remedy in the back of a broken-down wagon, all that impoverished shuck and jive. We considered this a windfall, Quentin, and so did you. A damn windfall," Augustas snapped. "If the big bosses want to control the valley, wonderful—because we get a cut of their action, and that's only for starters. Clients from them and my own patient will get squeezed to the last penny. Others'll wish to stay in town or build near the springs—think of the fees, the supplies and shipping we'll collect on once Elbow is under thumb. Stick with me, and you'll fart through silk."

"Still sounds too much like Santa Claus," Pollard grumbled.

There came a rap on the doors.

129

Augustas crossed to them, passing from Jessie's limited view. She heard a catch snap back and then heard Augustas greet suavely, "Ah, Mr. Muldow, so good of you to come at this hour. Please step in."

"Put 'er there, Doc. And howdy, Counselor, you got all our fooferaw ready?" The croaky voice was unmistakeable, and after the door closed, Jessie saw Augustas usher to his desk the sickly graybeard she'd met briefly that afternoon. Muldow was wearing a dressing gown and carpet slippers and was rasping, "You sold me, Doc. We both know I ain't got too many years left with alla mine dust I've swallered eatin' my lungs out. Been broke most my life, made my big strike too late to enjoy it, and ain't got no kin to leave it to. Yeah, I'd like to meet my Maker knowin' my money was helping poor folk."

"That's the spirit, Mr. Muldow. The fortune you have made in prospecting could not be devoted to a more splendid cause than the alleviation of suffering by those least able to afford medical attention. Here's my pen. Counselor, please show him where to sign."

Muldow sat in the desk chair, Augustas hovering on one side and Pollard on the other. Papers rustled. A pen scratched in silence. Then Muldow leaned back, coughed, and said, "I guess that's the last, ain't it? I'm feelin' plumb tuckered tonight."

"That's the lot," Pollard replied, refolding the papers and stuffing them in his pocket. "A most noble endowment, sir."

Augustas cleared his throat. "You'd better get right to bed, Mr. Muldow. Here, take this. It's your regular sleeping potion."

"Thanks, Doc." Mudlow rose and uncorked the bottle. "This stuff works mighty well. I sleep like a log—only next mornin' I feel sorta hungover, like I been on a toot." He swallowed and smacked his lips. "It don't taste the same as my reg'lar."

"A slight modification to help cure what ails you."

"Burnin' my throat!" Mudlow's voice was strangling, his eyes bulging as he staggered, sucking for air. "Wh– what'd you give me . . ." The weakening tones died off, and he started to collapse.

"Don't let him fall, Quentin," Augustas said sharply. "Get his arm. Good, now hold tight, and we'll carry him to his room."

"He must not've been too strong at that," Pollard remarked queasily. "Why couldn't we have waited and let nature take its course?"

"Certainly not. The old goat might have strung it out for five or ten more years, and he could've changed his will at any time. Strychnine's much better. It'll look as if he died in his sleep. We'll let a maid find him in the morning. C'mon, now, hurry!"

Squeamishly Pollard helped drag Muldow toward the doors. "I believe that I'll let Ol' Patches lead me home. I'll be up again tomorrow to hear the sad news so I can enter the will in probate."

"Fine, fine. You should write the obit tonight, though."

"I'll lay it on thick. Magnanimous miner, grateful to famous Dr. Augustas for saving his life, leaves his estate to the sanatorium where he spent his remaining years in comfort and joy." The pair of killers and their haul were beyond Jessie's sight, but she clearly heard Pollard yawn. "I can write such stuff in my sleep."

"Sounds like you just might," Augustas retorted testily.

There was a bumping of heels and then a hard slamming of the doors that sent the skeleton to dancing on its wire.

With rage in her heart at the cold-blooded poisoning of a defenseless old man, Jessie rose to her feet and silently backtracked to the closet door. Desperation gripped her as well, for she was all too aware that at best she had only one final chance to save Nehalem before Augustas chalked him up as the next victim.

131

She opened the door a crack, which gave her a view of the corridor to the foyer. It was empty and soundless. A second later, the door was shut behind her and she was striding innocently along as if she had an unquestioned right to be there. She was even smiling blithely at a passing attendant in the foyer. The attendant went up the central staircase, and again she was alone. It seemed almost too easy, luck favoring her all the way to the front door. Hereon, though, she had to use caution, for supposedly she was remaining in the house, and she maintained taut, edgy wariness as she turned the door handle and peeked outside.

Ahead, by the base of the veranda steps, was parked Pollard's buggy. Seen closer, his rig looked to be quite new and of good quality, with a longer rear bed than usual and with the swaybacked horse he'd called Ol' Patches nodding in its harness. Just beyond, another attendant was pacing the gravel driveway like a sentry. Jessie watched and waited for her chance to open the front door enough to slip through. When the buggy was between her and the walking guard, its top momentarily blocking his view, she scurried in a low hunch across the veranda, rolled under the railing, and dropped to earth behind the first line of bushes. She froze there in the darkness.

The guard returned, trudging within feet of where she crouched hidden, but showing no sign he suspected anything was amiss. Again he marched away, and once he was past the buggy, Jessie scuttled on hands and knees toward the corner of the house and then stopped as he came back. She kept moving in this manner on each far swing of his vigil until she was around the side and had reached the comparative safety of a shrub clump some fifty yards out from the house.

The windows, open for air, emitted vague noises of sleeping or retiring patients. Jessie caught no sound of attendants from inside, but heard their voices and boots off ahead and aside and glimpsed their shadowy figures as the search for her continued afield. Carefully gauging their locations, she picked her next spot and then took advantage of the ground's contours to crawl to it undetected. On she slithered from point to point, feeling her way to the black shelter of brush that skirted the track to the stable and corral.

There she crouched, wondering how best to proceed. Both the entry gate and stable area were guarded and lit, not that she had any intention of bracing either place. By the corral, however, she spied the only three men so far who were not outfitted in white—two wore range grubbies and were lazily saddling four horses while talking with the guards. The third man was sitting propped like a drunk against a corral post, and though Jessie could not see his face, she recognized him by his torn clothes: Uriah Nehalem.

Augustas had dispatched three killers, Jessie recalled, and she scouted for the missing partner of the two who were gearing the horses. Perhaps the man was still dallying with his soiled dove. Wherever he was, as soon as he arrived, Nehalem would be slung across a saddle and carried to his death. In anguish, she realized that now it was not how best, but how fast she could proceed that counted the most.

Yet Jessie forced herself to wait for those invaluable seconds when all heads were turned and attentions diverted. Even while seeing Pollard leave slowly in his buggy and knowing time was running out, she impatiently held back for the right moment.

The moment came as Pollard was approaching the entry gate. And it came suddenly, unexpectedly, nobody anticipating one of the men accidentally stubbing his cigar into the haunch of the horse beside him. The horse bucked squealing and began wheeling and scooting about with everyone chasing after it. A loud distraction, it was, and instantly Jessie sprinted across the open track and plunged on toward the limits of the sanatorium grounds.

Bush, trees, rocky swells of land helped conceal her hunkering form as she snaked quickly to the fence. Discovering a shallow depression nearby, she managed to wriggle under on her back. The barbed wire hummed, but the faint sound did not cause an alarm. She crept by a patch of dark tamarack and then rose and started climbing the heights. The ridge from which she'd first surveyed the sanatorium was not too far to her left, and she remembered that the lane to the entry gate had to flank this hill. If only she still had enough time, she prayed; if only Pollard was in no hurry and Ol' Patches was a plodder...

She ran full out, refusing to slow and thus risking a misstep, a fall, as she skimmed the rough slopes, skirting shale upthrusts and briar thickets. Whiplike branches slashed at her, thorny vines snagged her clothes, and once her ankle turned under her from a loose stone. On she sped, running, running—while sweat poured down her face and every breath rasped in her throat and stabbed her aching gut.

Abruptly she broke from low brush to the lane. She drew back to crouch off the shoulder, pretty sure the fork was just over the next rise beyond and the sanatorium was around the hill some distance behind. She was not sure at all if she had made it here before the buggy, but in any case she had to rest. Her lungs were heaving, and she was drenched with perspiration. Shortly her breath quieted. She mopped her face with her sleeve and then waited, regaining her wind while straining her ears for sounds of anyone approaching.

Nothing.

Jessie waited for what seemed like hours and was glumly concluding that Pollard had gotten by her when she caught the faint squeak of a wheel. She made ready, listening for it again. Then she saw the buggy's dark shape coming around the bend so slowly that at first she wondered if it was merely coasting to a halt. To term Ol' Patches a plodder was to put it mildly; he was dawdling along with nary a complaint from the driver.

She saw why as the buggy neared. Pollard was slouched in the upholstered seat, snoring asleep over the reins, overcome by weariness and, no doubt, his consumption of tonic. When Ol' Patches idled up to where Jessie waited, it did not shy or balk while she nimbly climbed aboard from the left side, squeezing in beside Pollard.

Pollard snorted and resumed his gargling snore.

Jessie took the reins away, eager to leave this narrow, hill-shrouded passage of lane before the killers with Nehalem appeared. The fork was preferable, she figured; it was a bit more open and moonlit, better for maneuvering the buggy and for shooting at any rider trying to escape. She slapped the reins to no avail. So she grabbed the whip from its socket and tickled a bony rump, which got Ol' Patches to crane his head with an injured look. The second time she laid the leather smartly, and her message sunk through. The horse quickened to a shuffling walk, the buggy swaying and the squeaky wheel chirping and rousting Pollard from his slumbers.

"What? Who?" he blurted, startled. "Where am I?"

"In your buggy, Counselor, going for a little ride."

"Miss Starbuck?" Staring at her, Pollard cleared his throat. "I thought you were at the sanatorium, m'dear."

"I was." Jessie applied the whip again, Ol' Patches objecting strenuously to trotting. She put the whip back in its socket and covertly drew her pistol. "But I couldn't very well stay in there and save Uriah Nehalem's life out here, could I?"

Pollard sat stunned. "H—how's that again?"

"You heard me as plainly as I heard you and Augustas meet."

"You what? Impossible! You couldn't have!"

"Watched you, too," Jessie replied conversationally, as

Ol' Patches strained. "Augustas doesn't shirk from petty matters like poisoning wealthy patients and ordering Nehalem and Abram Volner and heaven knows how many others murdered and so forth. He's chocked full of fine plans. Oh, no, you don't!"

Jessie clamped one hand over Pollard's fat wrist. With the other she whipped up her pistol and thrust it in his face. He stiffened, ogling its bore and gasping, "D–don't fire!"

"Don't move." Keeping her pistol trained, Jessie released his wrist and slid her hand inside his frock coat where, from an inner pocket, she withdrew a stubby hideout gun. She stuck it in her belt and then frisked Pollard for more weapons, not finding any but feeling his soft, blubbery flesh quivering with fear.

Pollard, however, was not without bluff. "Patently you are hallucinating our alleged meeting," he declared indignantly. "You are a sick woman, after all, who entered the sanatorium, and you are now making crazy accusations against two pillars of the community. It is purely your deranged word against ours. There is no evidence."

"You're forgetting, Counselor, the strychnine in Mr. Muldow and Augustas' less than illustrious past and his tapeworm elixir. You're also forgetting I'm no court of law. I'm Jessica Starbuck, the woman who's going to blow your brains out if you don't do exactly what I say, when I say."

Their eyes met and held. The buggy began rattling down the slope toward the fork, Jessie letting the silence grow until Pollard could stand the suspense no longer. His gaze broke, his eyes casting floorward and his lax lips gleaming as he sighed a great breath.

"What—What do you want me to do?"

"What do you think? Three men will be taking Nehalem along here on their way to kill him. I can't get near enough myself to snatch him away before they shoot him. But they're Tode's boys, and since you're part of the same litter, they'll let you move in close—with me scrunched down on the seat beside you."

"You are mad!" Pollard wrung his hands, whining. "You're alone, except for me, and I'm not built for such work, honestly."

Jessie didn't answer at once, hearing soft hoofbeats advancing on the lane behind them. "Riders. Maybe them. If they are, hail them when they come along and get the buggy close."

"But if they open fire, they may hit me—us."

"Then duck. Pollard, I'm through arguing. It's not a bullet you should fret about, but the hangman's noose because your only chance to save your skin is to help pin Augustas and Tode. Savvy?"

"I savvy." His voice was sickly.

The moon was high in the sky and its light streaked the clearing at the fork, though the surrounding shadows were black. Jessie turned the buggy so that the glow fell on Pollard's side, and she had no trouble in reining Ol' Patches to a dead stop.

On the lane from the sanatorium, horsemen loomed at the crest of the rise. They slowed, as if spotting the buggy, and then came on, pushing their horses. Jessie counted three of them leading a pack horse across which lay the drooping figure of Uriah Nehalem.

Chapter 14

Gripping her pistol with its hammer under one thumb, Jessie scrunched down in the buggy seat, shadowed by the rotund attorney.

"Remember, my first shot will go for you," she threatened, "if you try to warn those men or interfere with me in any way."

Pollard nodded, shaking like a leaf in the wind.

The front rider, a heavy man with a knife scar on his thick lips, called out, "Hiyuh, Pollard, yuh got woes?"

"Answer him." Jessie prodded. "A broken wheel or something."

"Yeah, my wheel, Curly. Hub's busted, I think," Pollard replied in a trembling voice. "I've just been sitting here waiting."

"Yuh're plunk in a pickle, ain't you?" Curly drawled, as he and his companions pulled in alongside the buggy. Then his grin widened to show stained teeth when he glimpsed the curve of Jessie's figure. "Why, you ol' lecher, out catting, too, eh?"

"No—I—She—" Pollard stammered, as Jessie brushed him while changing her position, and his voice ended in a groaning quaver.

The trio, suspicious by nature, frowned at Pollard. Yet they remained off their guard, Jessie figured, for they knew he was a friendly associate of Augustas and likely believed he was simply too boiled to speak properly. She shifted, her pistol gliding and hidden by Pollard's bulk, while Curly sidled closer to give her the eye.

"Can't fault your taste," he told Pollard, smiling roguishly at Jessie—then he gaped, his right hand clawing for his revolver as Jessie swung her pistol to cover him at point-blank range.

"Try," she said coldly.

Curly dropped his hand. "Pollard, call off your bitch."

"She's not my—I've nothing to do with—" Pollard choked, struggling for voice. "Please, just let her have what she wants."

"I'll take what I want," Jessie countered. "And I want Nehalem, the man you've got. But first I want you to light and shuck."

Curly, unbudging, spat a quick, defiant curse.

"She's only a dame." The second rider sneered.

"She can trigger her piece easy as a gent, Moe, and at them few feet, it'll do the aiming for her," the third rider cautioned, smarting angrily.

Jessie felt the tension and was aware they would only obey out of expediency, stalling and watching for a chance to strike. "I want Nehalem more than I don't want to shoot you. Climb down or fall down; the choice is yours." She clicked the hammer. *"Now."*

Curly dismounted grudgingly. His partners stayed asaddle as though reluctant to make any move without some sign that he would fight. Slowly, so none of his actions might be misconstrued, Curly unbuckled his gunbelt, and as it slid to the ground, he snarled, "Sister, yuh ain't gettin' much for your wants. Nehalem is dead."

In dismay, Jessie realized it might be true. Nehalem could have died from his beatings, or been stabbed at the sanatorium, or been killed by a muffled shot while on the lane. "We'll see. For your sake, I hope you're lying," she snapped, her facial muscles pulling taut. "Step away, now, and don't get cute."

Curly backed from his weapons, shrugging and with his

hands shoulder high, and bumped against his horse. The horse pranced skittishly, gave a nip, and got a clout in return. This seemed to provoke the second rider's horse. The rider, Moe, appeared to be wrangling to control his suddenly unruly mount, but Jessie suspected he was purposely trying to move around so they could catch her in a crossfire.

Grasping the buggy's top for support, she stretched and leveled her pistol at Moe. "Nice try, but far enough!"

The wolf-faced and unshaven killer reacted out of panic or contempt. Yelling "Damn her!" Moe made a fast draw, his bunched leather chaps pushing the holster up as he straddled his wheeling horse. It was like a signal to the other two men, Curly instantly diving for his dropped revolver, while the third rider unsheathed a sawed-off carbine.

Jessie fired, her hand unwavering. Her bullet struck Moe in the chest. His horse reared at the same time. He slumped, finished, and before he began sliding over the cantle of his saddle, Jessie was thrusting past Pollard to deal with the remaining pair of killers.

Lead searched the air where Jessie had been, and a quick glance showed her it had come from Curly, who was squatting by his gunbelt. She jumped from the buggy and swiveled up in a low crouch and shot back at the man. Her hasty bullet missed his vitals, but flicked Curly's inner shirt sleeve near his armpit and was sufficient to send him plunging in a roll under his shielding horse.

Then Jessie heard a wild cry, cut off by the hammering of hoofbeats as the third killer drove his mount toward her at a dead run. Behind her, Pollard was scrunching down in the seat, whimpering with fright. Curly's horse and the horse carrying Nehalem were pawing and snorting, and to the left, Moe's riderless mount was galloping aimlessly about. But Ol' Patches only shivered its hide and gazed around wondrously.

The rider squeezed off a shot with his shortened carbine, but his horse was dancing and spoiled his aim. His .50-caliber slug tore through the buggy top, and Pollard let out a squawk as though it had punched him in passing. The rider levered, but before he could fire, Jessie put a bullet in him. He doubled up in pain, triggering reflexively and drilling the top a second time.

It was too much for Pollard. "No! No! Stop!" he howled, scrambling upright in abject terror. Before Jessie could twist out of his way, he flopped from the buggy, knocking her aside.

Curly was setting for a shot and he tried too late to check himself. His bullet slammed into Pollard and spun Pollard staggering toward him, momentarily blocking his line of fire. "Git 'way!" he shouted and fired again and, once again, hit Pollard. In shocked, bewildered agony, Pollard blundered on, the force of his sagging body driving Curly backward. Soggily he fell, pinning Curly to the ground.

Jessie was using the instant to concentrate on the rider. He had started to go out of the saddle but was pulling himself upright, grimacing, lifting his carbine for another shot. Jessie triggered again. This slug punctured his heart. His horse gave a violent lunge and he pitched headlong to land with a hard, lifeless jolt.

A bullet clipped a stray wisp of her hair. She whirled to face Curly, who had shoved Pollard off and was now in a sitting position and aiming his revolver to shoot again. The slug that Jessie bored in Curly's breastbone slammed him back flat on the ground. He writhed weakly there, mouth gasping, eyes bulging, and fingers scratching at the dirt. He still hung onto his .45, however, and as Jessie fired again, Curly managed to snap off a shot that whistled past her cheek, its breath hot and vicious.

Then all grew very still.

Swiftly Jessie reloaded her pistol. The action had consumed mere seconds, yet they had been loud, sustained, explosive seconds. She doubted more killers were close— they'd have attacked by now—and perhaps the shooting hadn't carried as far as the sanatorium. But she couldn't count on that, for if the noise had been heard, it was bound to attract a rush of gunmen. She and Nehalem had to get away quickly, for it would be death to be caught here— and she wasn't even certain whether Nehalem was alive or not.

Slipping the pistol back behind her belt, she hurried to the horse carrying Nehalem. It shied from her touch, but acted tamer than the killers' mounts, and as she caught up its lead rope, Jessie had the fleeting thought that probably it and the gear were Nehalem's own, which would fit in with Augustas' scheme.

She felt Nehalem's face. Though badly beaten, it was warm, and a gentle movement of his shirt showed he still was breathing. Relief flooded through her. Curly had lied, no doubt, in an effort to throw her off. She walked the horse to the buggy. With her razor she slashed the ropes binding Nehalem to the saddle, then wrestled his heavy limp body across, and hoisted him onto the buggy seat.

The rest was a comparative breeze. Since she couldn't risk the saddle horses wandering home, she rounded them up and, using their saddle lariats, strung them to the rear of the buggy. The killers she dragged by their legs into concealing brush and rocks.

When she took hold of Pollard, he gave out a coughing moan. But he was beyond being wounded. She hunkered alongside him; he was dead and just didn't know it. Then, shuddering, he relaxed to sprawl inert.

Jessie grabbed his ankles and, while hauling him away, said, "Rest in peace, Counselor."

Returning to the buggy, she settled in with reins in hand and eyed Patches, who was watching her reproachfully. She picked up the whip, and saying, "Ol' Patches, you're

142

in for the run of your life," Jessie lavished its rump with a crackling swat.

Squealing, the horse vaulted three feet and romped off at a frothy trot. Jessie peered behind to check if the saddle mounts were trailing in good order. They were. The fork lay pristine in the moonlight, displaying no signs of the recent carnage other than a few bloodstains soaked in the dirt. Killing had been done, though, and she had done it. In self-defense, true, but that could not fill the hollow sadness of regret. Yet Jessie felt no remorse, only pity that there were men like those who needed dying and relief that none had escaped to carry the alarm back to Augustas.

At the main road, Jessie turned reluctantly townward. Nehalem kept swaying and muttering, often drifting close yet never quite back to consciousness. She wished he would; she needed directions to get him home, knowing only that his ranch lay to the southwest. She'd muddle there on her own, she supposed, for she was not about to stop in town to ask. In fact, she would've preferred to bypass Elbow altogether, but her strange caravan prevented her from taking any cross-country short cuts.

Reaching town, Jessie maneuvered along a series of alleys, hearing the hoopla and tinny music spill from the main street. She passed the rear of the law office, still with the gaping hole in its wall, and after that Nehalem began to stir. He straightened halfway before his strength deserted him; then he slumped low again, panting, and blearily eyed Jessie.

"Don't pinch me," he wheezed. "I fears I'm dreamin'."

Jessie smiled. "You're awake and out of the sanatorium."

"I am, so I am." Woozy, he gazed around. "Why, we're in Elbow, ain't we, and ain't this Pollard's rig? How the devil did you manage it? Don't ya reckon we oughta tell Sheriff Renwick?"

"Later—in due time. You need attention, Uriah. Tell

143

me how to find your ranch; then I'll spell out everything you missed."

Nehalem was glad to comply, and shortly they were south beyond the Sangrar Wash bridge, heading west on his ranch trail. En route, Jessie recounted how she rescued him after fleeing to the roof and then overhearing Augustas and Pollard. The death of Muldow, the motive for murdering Nehalem, the planned raid on his spread tonight, and the one on the Box L last night—Jessie left out nothing except how the cartel was involved, Nehalem having enough to digest as it was. She stressed instead how, as she put it, "Sheep smell to a cowman like you, and they used your feuding as a cover-up for a big land grab."

Appalled, Nehalem sputtered, "Raids! Holdups! Killin's! All so's they can buy cheap from scared folk and widders and orphans!" He stiffened, pointing ahead where the sky glowed red with fire. "Migawd, Tode's gang must've struck me like you said they would. Sure, get me to feudin', then get rid of me, same's they got rid of Thad Latimer and Kessler, too, I betcha." He sank back, passing a hand over his battered face, weak and sick from the realization.

Ol' Patches slowed, looking back in hopes it'd shaken the fiend riding atail. Jessie laid a spank, as she had been doing now and again, and the horse promptly resumed a more reasonable pace. Yet it could be hurried only so much. And time was speeding by.

Finally, at a whip-enticed run, they rolled into the ranch yard. The surprised hands congregated around the buggy, while Ol' Patches dozed off, and Ki and Hodel helped out Nehalem, who was too wobbly to stand alone. A sharp wail erupted from Faith as she saw her father's sagging body propped between the two men.

Nehalem managed a wink. "Don't bury me yet, child."

"We better get him inside," Jessie said. "He needs care."

Ki nodded and with Hodel he began the slow task of carrying and supporting Nehalem into the ranch house. Faith pushed past them to light a parlor lamp hastily and was starting for a hallway when Nehalem growled that the couch would do fine and not to bother Mama.

But Mrs. Nehalem was already aroused. "Now what's all the commotion?" she called. Then she and Hope appeared from the hall. "Uriah!" With an anxious clutching of their robes, they hastened to where he was stretching out on the long, overstuffed couch. "You're a sight. You're a wonder to be alive! Oh, thank the Lord, you are!"

"Now, now, dear, I look more banged up than I am."

His wife was not mollified. "We'll fetch the doctor—"

"Dagnabit, where d'you think I've been? That charlatan and his dirty hounds took me prisoner and were gonna kill me!"

"Oh, no, Uriah, not sweet Doc Augustas."

"Sweet! He's a homicidal quack, plottin' to gobble up this whole valley and turn it into a gigantic sanatorium swindle. And cahootin' with him is Froggy Tode to handle the strong-armin', plus Quentin Pollard to crank out publicity and shyster the legalities."

Jessie whispered to Ki, "And bankrolled by you-know-who. The place serves as a hideaway for their members."

Ki gave her a knowing glance and then said to Nehalem, "It makes sense, Uriah, and ties in with the raid here tonight. It was led by Tode."

"Right, Dad," Hope confirmed insistently. "The Box L had nothing to do with it, so don't go roaring blame at the Latimers."

"I believe you, child." His face twisted in a sour smile. "Reckon I'm due to eat considerable crow to those two sheepherders."

"Listen, we haven't much time to nail Augustas cold," Jessie said in an urgent voice. "Ki, ride to the Box L. Tell Glenn to have everyone dress scruffy like outlaws, pack lots of weapons and ammunition, and sneak in close to the sanatorium's main entry by four-thirty the latest. No, have him ask the men. They're not paid to risk their lives, and it won't be held against them if they refuse to go. Uriah, do you think any of your crew might be willing to get shot at?"

Hodel spoke for his boss. "The Box L ain't paying our scores for us. We got a right to be in on your raid, and every hand here'll be itching to stiff the Doc a dose of his own stampede medicine."

Jessie shook her head. "No, no wild charging in. It'll mean certain death for many innocent patients and probably for all of us. We'll be outnumbered to begin with and be cut to pieces before we rush the barbed wire fence and the thick walls of the buildings."

"So we trick our way in dressed like Tode's henchmen."

"Yes, Ki. The entrance guards should be removed," Jessie said, "but otherwise I figure the inside gunmen can be fooled long enough for you to close in on the main house where Augustas is."

Nehalem nodded. "Smart. 'Cept why so early in the mawnin'?"

"It's when people are most relaxed, sleep soundest, and it's the soonest we can get set," Jessie explained. "After daybreak, Augustas is apt to discover reasons his game is over, and he'll hit the wind. Also, he knows where Tode and his bunch are camped in the hills, and they can't be left to run loose. That reminds me. Sheriff Renwick should be invited to attend our surprise party."

"He's liable to stop it, not join it," Ki warned.

"True. We've no proof. But I spotted a number of crooks staying at the sanatorium, so the threat of us going in to make citizen arrests could bring him," Jessie advised. "No posse, though; word might leak to those we're after. Just the sheriff, to make it legal."

"Renwick will come," Nehalem pledged. "I'll go get—"

"To bed," his wife declared. "Norm can ride to town."

Nehalem grumbled, but not very hard, and then said, "Well, with or without the sheriff along, I say go for it. Ain't nothin' to be lost by giving your plan a twirl, Miz Starbuck. What's your next step?"

"To return to the sanatorium before they learn I'm on the prowl. Y'see, the gate guards must be dealt with from the inside," she replied. "If the horses we brought aren't too tuckered, I'll ride one back and leave it hidden. If found, it'll cause questions, but at least it won't carry a brand that'll give any answers. Anyway, come four-thirty I'll have that entrance open for you."

★

Chapter 15

On Curly's mustang, Jessie left the ranch and hurried straight overland to the sanatorium. She detoured onto the lane, passed the fork to make sure its clearing was undisturbed, and near where she had intercepted Pollard cut into the brush and dismounted. She tethered the mustang on a long rope so it could graze and hiked the rest of the way to the depressed spot at the fence.

The sanatorium looked dark and quiet in the small hours. The same number of men were patrolling the grounds and guarding the gate, where a lantern gleamed in the night. Jessie squirmed under the wire and made her cautious return to the main house, gratified that for the moment some cloud wisps were veiling the stars and moon. In crouching sprints, she wormed from cover to cover toward the side of the house, ducking behind the bordering shrubbery when she reached it and flattening while two men marched past. Then she was up and scuttling inside.

When finally she closed the door of her room, she felt done in, run to a frazzle. Pouring water into the bowl, she began to wash. Okay, she won the first skirmish, she thought while she scrubbed, but only because Augustas wasn't aware yet of her fight. At his command through Tode was a powerful gang, plus a highly tuned sensitivity to danger where it concerned his safety. Once he caught the slightest whiff of peril, she reminded herself as she pocketed extra ammunition, he would throw all his muscle at his opponent, while he snuck his skin out through some escape hatch.

On the dresser was a spoon and an amber tonic bottle— her medicine prescribed by Augustas. That worried her, for whenever Tyrone had delivered it, she hadn't been here. She wondered if the receptionist had taken notice of her absence, perhaps had reported it . . . but it was too late to worry, to wonder, to do anything about it. Curious, though, she uncorked the bottle and took a tentative sip. A liquid torch flowed down her gullet, detonating a charge in her stomach that sent her shuddering convulsively.

"Jesus, it must be a hundred and fifty proof!" she gasped.

Fortified by a second sampling, she left her room to go back outside. This time she went out strutting, inviting attention.

The men were happy to oblige. The first guard she encountered ogled her, licking his lips. "Who're you, babe?"

"Delores," Jessie said, batting her lashes.

"Yeah? Delores what?"

"Just Delores. Last names get in the way of friendships."

The guard snickered. "Whatcha doin' out here so late?"

"I'm meeting Curly. He's coming with a bunch of the boys."

"Yeah? I hadn't heard such. How would you know?"

"Guess where my ears are," she retorted sassily and sashayed on to spread the message that some of Tode's gang were due very soon.

There was a suspicious grayness, the false dawn, in the sky by the time Jessie had gossiped her way down near the main entry. She carefully kept out of view of its wayside shed, though every so often she heard or caught glimpses of the gate guards inside. The posted lantern cast a yellow

149

glow around the entrance, but now it seemed to appear dimmer—no doubt due to the softening darkness, Jessie decided.

When she was sure nobody was looking, she ducked among rocks behind a building and then eased to the fence. From there she began a noiseless crawl through the scrub and stone toward the rear of the wayside shed. She snaked across the last few open yards and then squatted silently by its back corner. She drew her pistol, tensing and licking dry lips. The driveway clearing in front of the shed was wide and dangerously bare, and she held her breath as she broke into a fast leap forward along the fence side of the shed.

Her mouth pursed taut in a merciless line, Jessie pivoted and plunged into the open front of the shed. "Freeze, you two!" she hissed, training her pistol.

The men, outfitted in white, turned and smiled at her.

The expression on Jessie's face became one of utter bewilderment. "Ki! Glenn! What in heaven . . . ?" She stared at them, started to speak again, closed her lips instead, and continued to stare.

"We thought we'd save you some trouble," Glenn Latimer said cheerily. "We can pass for the guards better'n you."

"Thanks, but what a shock! I'd no inkling—you were like ghosts. Where're the guards now—ghosts, too?"

"No, the sheriff's protecting them from that fate. They're tied in their skivvies a ways back with him and our guys," Ki replied.

Glenn added, "Renwick warned us that the doc and the sanatorium are popular hereabouts. It's our roundup, but if we tangle our twine, we get full blame and he'll clap us in chains."

"It figures. Whatever happens, he'll get the credit," Jessie observed wryly. "And it may go either way, I suspect. There's been no alarm, I think, and Augustas' men aren't alert as they might be. But they aren't asleep, either, and are everywhere. Luckily they're wearing white, so we can tell them apart from the patients."

"Our boys, all fourteen of 'em, are aware we don't bloody any innercents," Glenn assured her. "Well, it's time I got back to 'em."

"And for me to head to the main house again. I want to be able to get at Augustas before someone smells a rat. What about you, Ki?"

"I'm staying to play gatekeeper. Go on, now, go!"

A quick peek out, then Jessie and Glenn slipped from the shed. "Have the men concentrate on the house," she told him as they dived along the side. "This is a snake pit, and Augustas is the head. If we fail to chop him up, he'll wriggle away and soon grow a new body."

They parted, Glenn angling to where he and Ki had been crossing the fence and Jessie darting on her hazardous return. Once there, she began her tart's act again, brazenly walking and even whistling as added distraction to cover any noise Glenn might make.

While on her way, two guards came and one demanded, "Cut it out."

"But I'm happy. Curly and the guys will be here soon."

"So we heard," the other said. "I don't care. You're disturbin' sleepers. You best get to bed, too, before you land in trouble."

"Why, bed's where I land most in trouble." Saucily she smiled at one guard and winked at his companion. Yet, as she continued to saunter toward the house, Jessie felt grimly anxious. Several details, any one of which might have tipped the shrewd, tricky Augustas, preyed on her mind. A slip, and he could still very well elude her.

A drum of hooves sounded on the lane, and the patrolling gunmen grew swiftly alert. Jessie quickened her pace, though she glanced over her shoulder to see if her ruse would work. A knot of riders loped into view and pulled up at the entry gate. From the wayside shed stepped a white-clad gate guard, his features too shadowed to be clearly visible. He gave the riders a friendly wave, unlocked the gates, and swung them wide open. The gunmen around near Jessie noticeably relaxed, lulled by the riders' disreputable appearance and the gate guard's obvious acceptance of them.

The riders entered the grounds and, while Ki locked the gates behind them, moved nonchalantly toward the main house. Hats tugged low, one hand on reins and the other casually toting a rifle or brushing a holstered revolver, they slouched, looking weary and indifferent. Yet inwardly, Jessie felt sure, they were watchful and determined. The Nehalem crew had joined in common cause with Box L men who mere hours before were considered their bitter enemies.

As they approached, the duped gunmen grinned and slackened their weapons, forgetting the gate guard—who had vanished, leaving his white outfit in the shed. "Where's Curly?" a gunman called out. "He's gotta tomato waitin', jus' slaverin' to get plucked!"

Jessie sprang through the front door, hearing the first shout of alarm. "Somethin' funny here!" She dashed down the foyer for the office, while from outside burst yells of surprise and warning.

"Hey, this ain't none o' Froggy's bunch!"

"Look out!"

"A trap!"

Guns rose to shoot the riders, but Augustas' renegade attendants, as vicious and callous a breed as Tode's outlaw thugs, were caught napping. The combined ranch crews, anticipating this moment, already were sweeping up their weapons and surging in like a tidal wave. With cries of shock and pain, the gunmen dropped notions of attack and turned to defend their own exposed hides, scurrying for cover and digging in while hastily firing back.

As the sanatorium grounds erupted in an inferno of pounding boots, rearing horses, and blasting guns, Jessie tore into the anteroom that served as the receptionist's office. The side door on her left, she recalled, was to Augustas' professional quarters; the door on her right, therefore, quite likely led to his private chambers, where he'd probably be at this hour. She veered right, pistol up.

The tips of her fingers were almost touching the handle when suddenly the door was flung open. There stood the receptionist, Tyrone, draped in a cerise lounging robe, his nose jutting, his eyebrows arching in a snitty expression of annoyance and inquiry.

She stuck her foot against the door. "Is Augustas in there?"

His eyebrows tented higher. "I think you should leave."

Jessie wasn't interested in Tyrone's thoughts. She grabbed his lapels, shaking him. "Where is Augustas?" she snapped.

"Help!" Tyrone screamed. "Oh, help me, I say!"

There came an answering yell and steps sounding from overhead, from the central staircase, and from the foyer. Jessie thrust hard, sending Tyrone sprawling with robe aflutter, and leaped for the office doorway. Beyond, the foyer was a crush of aroused attendants pouring in from corridors and down the stairs. Some were plunging out the front door, but most were readying to bolt it and fight from inside, and a handful were heading toward her with carbines in hand.

Jessie kicked the office door shut and latched it. Wonderful—she was locked in, the hands were being locked out, and there was a hornet's nest between. Swiveling, she saw that Tyrone had regained his feet and was pointing a .32 at her.

"I shall fire!" he threatened shrilly.

For an expressionless instant, Jessie regarded the pistol in his wavering fist. "You shan't," she declared and rushed him.

Tyrone fired. Jessie felt a twitch at her jacket. The small caliber slug hit the office door behind her and raised a howl from the other side. Blanching, Tyrone spun and bounded through the side doorway. Jessie chased him, while a salvo of heavy carbine bullets began raking the oak panels of the office door.

Slamming and latching the side door, Jessie made a swift scan of the room. It was very dimly lit by a single candle, yet she could discern it was equal in size to the examination room and had a big bed instead of a big desk and a similar set of doors that were swung partially open. She didn't spot Augustas, but his rattled receptionist was cowering by the bed, trying to steady an aim on her. She shot at him, purposely missing by inches.

"Where's Augustas? I want him, not you!"

Tyrone was a disbeliever. With a squeak, he frantically scuttled the short stretch to the doors and disappeared outside.

Jessie sprinted across and through the doors. Then she stopped, giving up pursuit and glimpsing his black silhouette scampering away.

The rear was pooled in gloom, the house windows all dark, the sky murky as it phased from moonlight to dawn. And the area was embroiled in death, perhaps less intensely than the turmoil in front, but a killing field nonetheless. Guards and attendants were running hunched over, weapons blazing in their grips. Their white shirts and trousers outlined them harshly and mercilessly. The hands were quick, hazy figures darting spread out and elusive. The air quivered from their deafening exchange of gunfire.

Into this savagery fled Tyrone, brandishing his pistol, bare legs palely flashing, his cerise robe flapping like a cape in a breeze. The hands ignored him, thinking he was a patient; the gunmen targeted him, not knowing or caring what he was. Tyrone took five more prancing strides before he was hit. He fell shrieking; the man who plugged him was abruptly plugged in return.

A slug whined past Jessie's ear. Hastily she dipped back in through the doors, convinced that wherever else Augustas might be, he surely wasn't out there. She heard the cry of another victim—then a closer and more brutal roar as a burst of carbine bullets riddled the side door. Realizing the gunmen from the foyer must have breached the office, Jessie wheeled just in time to see the door latch assembly fragment and plummet to the floor.

The door swung open. Four burly gunmen, jostling one another with their long-barreled guns, began spilling in while trying to shoot. Desperately Jessie triggered into their midst. Her bullet snuffed the life of the nearest man, who grunted and toppled back against his companions, disrupting their aim that much more.

With their fusillade swirling around her, Jessie dived behind the bed, making a wild swipe at the candle to extinguish it. The candle tipped over. The room was dashed into blackness. Crouching, Jessie snapped a shot at a gunman still in the doorway, his form looming against the softer dark of the office beyond. He crumpled with hands pressing his wound, rolling in agony and thrashing his legs.

But Jessie's shot betrayed her position, and the remaining two gunmen opened up with a broadside. The pillows spewed feathers, the bedspread squirmed like a thing alive, and the box springs twanged from bullets burrowing through the mattress. Trapped, Jessie crawled rapidly up the bed, hoping to worm behind its thick wooden headboard, and bumped into the chamber pot. It sloshed and reeked, but she ignored that. Hefting it by its handle, she flung it overhand toward the far corner. It sailed and crashed, its porcelain shattering loudly, and the gunmen reacted relfexively by blasting away at it. Jessie reared and shot them both.

One man caught a slug through the top of his skull and died instantly, his brain blown apart. He sunk without a sound, without so much as a twitch. The other man lurched awry as though struck in the pectoral or the shoulder. Face contorting, he was swinging his carbine to deal with her when he uttered a taut groan and sagged.

"Don't shoot," he panted. "I'm pegged. I quit." Then he collapsed, blood gushing from his mouth, and lay still.

At that moment, from the front of the house, came the sound of smashing glass. There were yells, a rash of gunfire. That, Jessie guessed, would be the hands breaking in a window. Figuring they would draw any gunmen away from here, she righted, relit the candle, and then searched the room while reloading her pistol.

The furniture was of carved woods, massive and expensive. The bed was a cavernous canopy affair sporting frilly lace, scrolled posts, and a headboard of gilded cherubs. Crimson drapes framed the doors and on the floor was an immense rug of Indian design. The adjoining bathroom was a splendor of white enamel and hand-painted tiles. It had a tub the size of a small lily pond.

This, Jessie decided, was not Tyrone's bedroom. No receptionist could afford it. No, this was Augustas' personal chambers, and they certainly reflected a sybaritic side to him that she never would have dreamed existed.

Problem was, Augustas wasn't in the room.

She slipped out of the office, wary as a hunting panther, and prowled through the examination room. She did not find Augustas. He could be hiding anywhere, she thought, and she'd have to comb the house, including the roof. Yet she started to fear that he had managed to make his escape, while Tyrone was busy delaying her.

She left the examination room, hearing the defiant

snarls of the gunmen barricaded in the house. But the hands were inside as well, their blazing muzzles spitting lead and fire. Augustas' hired troops had suffered heavy casualties during the initial surprise of the attack, and now they were battling the assault of pistols and knives. If the hands had been gritty and courageous when their ranches had been raided, they were absolute terrors in exacting their revenge on any gunman.

And yet, for all their ferocity, the hands honored their pledge to Jessie to avoid wholesale butchery. Patients were constantly warned to stay out of this, to stay in their rooms or tents, a common sense order very few thought to challenge. Only those wearing white were figured fair game; those waving white were taken prisoner. When forced to, they killed implacably, but they tried to gain the drop or to wound if given a choice.

Norm Hodel's rifle was crackling steadily, aiming accurately. A gunman's hat was knocked from his bald head. Glenn and Dwight Latimer formed a crossfire team and were prowling from room to room, routing gunmen and demanding their surrender. Ki was pressed to the foyer staircase, which was rampant with strife, but it was central to both floors should Jessie need help or Augustas pop up. A pig-eyed man's leg buckled as he was about to trigger; he sat down hard on the steps and blinked stunned at the *shuriken* stuck in his calf. Another clutched his shoulder, yelping in pain, Ki's embedded dagger having driven the fight from him.

The conflict raged on. Despite their seeming disadvantage in numbers and tactics, the crewhands continued increasing their toll. The surviving gunmen resisted stubbornly, but began to consider their old owlhoot motto: If the going gets rough, haul ass.

Ironically, though not surprisingly, it was the cartel criminals guesting at the sanatorium who were first to break. Most were unarmed and not gunslingers by trade.

157

Besides, this was not their war. It was bound to bring the law—indeed, it had already; a mustachioed grizzly with a badge on his vest could be seen storming about, trying to pacify the patients and referee the combatants. So, packing and scrambling, the nervous ones dashed for the stable, hoping to catch a fast horse out of the place.

Their exodus set off a chain reaction. Gunmen leaped out of doors and windows in a panicked retreat, fleeing headlong in every direction by vaulting into saddles or scattering on foot for the haven of the hills. They promptly collided with the barbed wire fence and the locked entry gate. The result was a costly crushing of those afoot. Horses shied, rearing, stomping, and spooking.

Consistently harassed by the crewhands, the demoralized gunmen and crooked guests stampeded around the fringes or bolted back toward buildings. They burrowed into hiding spots about the grounds, and sought cover behind doors, under floors, in dark nooks and crannies. But the crewhands were persistent, flushing and chousing them. As one after another was captured, guns and other weapons were collected. The captured were driven to the horse corral, where they were temporarily penned.

Ki and Glenn Latimer were securing the hands of two prisoners when Jessie hastened over. She looked worried, almost distraught, and Glenn tried to cheer her with a triumphant grin. "We ain't got it finished yet, Jessie, but I reckon we got a good start on it."

"Well, I don't. I can't locate Augustas."

Her failure sobered them. Tersely Ki said, "Wait here a minute." He hustled the prisoners across to the corral.

Norm Hodel happened to be there. After a brief word with Ki, he hurried back with him, his hamlike hands hooked in his belt and determination in his eyes. "Okay, let's go find that buzzard."

The action having spread widely outside, the house was left relatively calm, as if in the hushed aftermath of a storm. The four stirred it noisy again, alarming already frightened servants and patients as they scoured it from roof to cellar. But Augustas was not there. Frustrated, Jessie did not wish to give up, recalling her own words about a snake growing a new body. Yet after their exhaustive hunt, she had to admit her quarry had eluded her.

"Damn Augustas!" she swore, venting her wrath. "He's slipped the noose somehow. Smelled trouble and took it on the lam."

She would not—could not—rest with Augustas at large.

Chapter 16

Depressed, the foursome returned to the corral where the hands were still herding newly caught prisoners. To compound their misery, Sheriff Renwick steamed over, his face crimson and glowering as if he were suffering from ten ingrown toenails.

"Why," he growled, "did you have to go back to the house?"

Jessie shrugged. "We were looking for Augustas."

"Stand in line with a ton o' patients. Except, they want to anoint him with oil and polish his halo—while they crucify us."

"They jus' dunno the truth yet," Hodel said. "Augustas posed good as a great doctor. He hoaxed all o' us in the valley, so, of course, he'd hoax the gen'ral public what swallows his phony tracts and treks a long ways to be cured. Ain't that so, Ki?"

Ki nodded without comment as he scanned the prisoners milling about the makeshift stockade. Some were bleeding from wounds. Their features were uniformly glum, though their eyes ranged the gamut from scared to sullen to hateful. His interest was piqued by one gunman who was trying to roll a cigarette with a bad case of jitters. Lanky, balding, and with jug ears and a scrawny neck, the man concentrated on his smoke as if suffering a nicotine fit, finally fumbling it together and lighting it. While watching, Ki heard the sheriff speak.

"Aw'ri', you go tell 'em the truth, Norman. Judas

knows I can't. And they're no general public patients, neither. They're a committee of moguls and gran' dames. They roasted me alive once already and'll do it again, thanks to your ransacking the joint a second time." Renwick tugged his mustache, scowling at the four. "I hate bein' called a nincompoop, a frontier heathen. I hate worser when one politician or another is a personal buddy and'll hear of the outrage. It sounded like a St. Louis stockyard auction, and I didn't have any answers to shut 'em up with. Well, I want some, plenty of 'em, and right pronto!"

"Fine," Jessie replied blandly. "So do we."

The sheriff stiffened as if scalded. "You better have 'em to give. If you can't, if this's some prank played on decent folk hereabouts, I'll give 'em all of you—tarred and feathered!"

"The answers are in the corral." Jessie patted Renwick's gnarled fist. "Those attendants know enough to prove the operation is a fraud. Plus, Dodge City records show that seven, eight years ago, Augustas was arrested as Doc Terwilliger, hawking an elixir, while Tode shilled a crooked card game. Abram Volner lived there then, and when he came here, he recognized the doc. So he was killed and dumped to make it look like banditry. Anyway, the corral also holds some so-called patients who're wanted criminals. Send fliers and bulletins—"

"Ma'am, I'd be sacked long before I got those answers," the sheriff cut in crabbily. "Look at 'em, they're coyotes who won't volunteer nothing. By the time I could trace who did what where an' when, I'd have bankrupted the territory in detention and postal fees."

Ki nodded as he walked to the corral gate. "Yes, we need the answers here and now, so we need to get them here and now."

"And fast, if you're gonna get off the hook."

"The surest way off a hook is to put someone else on

161

it." Ki responded with a tight grin. He went inside the corral and across to the lanky man he'd watched rolling a smoke. "Come with me."

"Oh, yeah—*Ow!*" the man cried, as Ki levered his arm behind his back and pushed him forward. "Lay off! I sprained my shoulder."

"Too bad Doc Augustas isn't here to treat you," Ki retorted, propelling the man to the gate. While heading out, Ki told the hand who was posted there, "Pass the word for everyone who can be spared to come and join our party. It might prove educational."

The party was waiting and curious, and when Ki marched the man over, Renwick frowned quizzically. "Okay, so who's this?"

Ki squeezed. The man found voice. "Evans! Arne Evans."

"Arrest him," Ki said. "He helped abduct Uriah Nehalem."

Everybody was astounded except Arne Evans, who instantly got belligerently indignant. "You're loco! I'm a law-abiding citi—"

"Quiet," Renwick snapped and he eyed Ki. "Any proof?"

"I found where Uriah was waylaid. Four riders, the prints are clear. Faith saw them, too." From his vest, Ki took a butt he'd retrieved from the arroyo. "Also the cigarettes of a heavy smoker."

"Lotsa people smoke!" Evans countered. "It don't mean—"

"Pipe down," Renwick barked, inspecting the butt.

Ki said casually, "The paper has blue stripes." Then abruptly he spun Evans around, rifling the startled man's shirt pocket for his tobacco and papers. "And this's the same brand, Blue Ribbons."

Evans was livid. "Gimme; them's mine! I demand my rights—"

"Clamp it!" Renwick bellowed. "This here's evidence."

"Naw, I'd like to hear him talk." Norm Hodel was grinding fist against palm, his eyes burning like dark coals in his rigid face. "Talk and talk about his pards and who done the beatin's."

"Not me, you got the wrong boy. I don't know nuthin'."

Facing Hodel to snarl his denial, Evans could not see Ki give Hodel a broad wink. Hodel caught it; so did Jessie, who smiled to herself. "Evans," Ki began affably, "you have the sort of neck that should produce a long, strong voice, but I haven't heard it."

Turning to Ki, Evans bared his teeth like a wolf at bay.

"The problem is your neck is bent, I figure, putting kinks in the root of your tongue, and it ought to be straightened out," Ki said. "Norm, I think perhaps if his neck was given a stretch at the end of a rope, it might just loosen his tongue. Don't you?"

Hodel peeled his lips in a nasty, mirthless grin. Renwick moved as if to intervene, but Jessie restrained him with a hand and a flashing signal from her eyes, so he hesitated, seeming unsure what to do next. Glenn appeared slightly taken aback by Ki's suggestion, yet not so much against it that he was willing to defend Evans.

And Hodel followed through by glancing at the Nehalem cowhands who had gathered around. "Fetch a lariat. We'll hang him high."

Arne Evans gave a panicked yell and attempted to break away, only to be overpowered immediately by two of the burly Nehalem crew. He tried again to wrench free when the rope was brought and given to Hodel. During the scuffling distraction, Jessie whispered to the sheriff. Hodel began to fashion a hangman's knot, while Evans struggled impotently and stared with terrified eyes.

"Sheriff, stop them!" Evans begged. "Make them stop!"

"Why, sure," Renwick replied with yawning disinterest. "Of course, a lynch mob is a powerful, terrible force to

163

buck, me bein' one lone man against all these well-meanin' friends and neighbors."

Evans let out a tormented moan, his defiance showing signs of weakening. He looked around frenziedly, as though trying to see some way to escape, and saw only an encirclement of stony, merciless faces.

"Don't do it," he pleaded. "Dead men can't talk."

Hodel chuckled. "Live ones who won't are good as dead."

"But if I . . . How do I know you'll not do it, anyway?"

"Our word. That's all and that's sufficient." Ki's voice was icy and low. "You'll have your chance to face judge and jury and beat a legal hanging. Hold your tongue here and you have no chance."

Evans' tongue caressed his dry lips, his eyes transfixed on the noose. Hodel was crafting it, not just tying it, and his exacting deliberations became a lingering horror. Evans could not withstand it, and his shoulders slumped as he surrendered, ready to clutch at any chance to save his own neck. "It's a deal."

Jessie gave a soft, satisfied sigh as Evans started to talk. Once uncorked, he jabbered like a politico, mostly confirming what she already knew and adding minor details but no startling revelations. Her eyes shifted from him, swept the sour glares of his fellow prisoners, and read the reactions on the faces of the surrounding men, especially the sheriff. They were listening to a man confessing for his life, exposing his crimes without thought of lying, but with the truth that comes of desperation . . . And Jessie knew that they knew they were hearing the truth.

"Skunk-blooded bunch of sidewinders," Renwick declared, when Evans lapsed quiet to catch his breath. "I got my answers, okay."

"But we don't have ours yet," Ki said evenly, and he faced Evans with a trace of a crooked smile. "This isn't an

164

asking; it's a telling. You are going to lead us to wherever Augustas is hiding."

"I don't know," Evans said plaintively. "I swear it!"

"All right, then to Tode's camp."

After a moment's hesitation, Evans nodded. "I'll do it," he murmured. "If I gotta choose 'tween Tode or me . . ."

Ki turned to Latimer and Hodel. "Let's get hustling. Tode's camp was next anyway, but I think Augustas may well have fled there to alert him and link up. They could pull stakes anytime, and they're bigger fish than any last few we'd catch here. Have your crews arm and saddle up. We'll leave the wounded men here with the bound prisoners till we can send for them. What's our tally?"

"Four dead, five wounded, nine able," Latimer replied.

"Better scrub that to eight," Renwick said gruffly. "This's one jaunt we won't want Miz Starbuck on. Won't be woman's work."

Jessie did not respond in words. She just looked at him.

The sheriff looked at her look, fidgeted, yanked his mustache, and then sighed that sigh of men plagued by women. "Hmmm. Yes. Maybe if real careful and stayin' down . . ." Hastily he changed subjects, frowning authoritatively. "There're differences from raidin' here and raidin' a known fugitive's roost, and one is that Tode gets raided by a proper posse. So consider yourselves deputized. Also spread around that nobody's to lynch Arne Evans. He's in my custody. His only chance for leniency will be when we testify he helped us."

Hodel nodded, but warned Evans, "I'm carrying my rope, and if you try a double-cross, I'll string you to the nearest anything."

"There'll be none of that. No need," Renwick said grimly. "Evans, if you bamboozle us into a trap, I'll shoot you first. Savvy?"

Evans nodded and backed away. He understood.

Soon, with the broken-spirited gunman giving directions, the posse swept eastward across the valley plain and passed beyond the town to the Sierra Estrellas. From the low foothill cluster of rocks and arroyos, they climbed a twisty maze of trails while the dawning sun rose brassy and waxen. Then they traversed upland ridges and dipped through raviness laced with a webwork of paths. It was wild, harsh terrain, befitting a hide-out for criminals.

Along about midmorning, they emerged into a steeply sloped, scrubby ravine that resembled most all the ravines that had come before it. Arne Evans found it distinctive enough to call a halt. His voice was low. "The camp ain't far, now. Keep things quiet."

Cautiously they moved on, Evans and the sheriff riding point. After short stretches of several faint trails, Evans chose one that was deviously hidden by shadowed and sunlit walls of bush and boulder. It ended only a half mile or so farther on at Tode's encampment.

Evans cut them off the trail before the camp. Leading their horses, they crept through thickening growth to where they could see without being seen, able to hear as they neared the faint noises of men. At last, by cautiously parting a row of brush, they could view the shielded canyon in which the camp lay. Its sides were rather sharply banked and had been undercut by some ancient flood. The shelves offered shelter for men and equipment. Tented tarpaulins gave additional protection. Saddles and other gear could be seen, and men were loafing about taking naps or drinks, or playing cards, or broiling food over a low, smokeless fire.

"Odd, I don't see any sentries," Renwick commented.

"Naw, you won't see none on the high points," Evans responded. "Tode has 'em patrolling lower 'round the walls."

Ki asked, "Counting them, how many should be down there?"

"About thirty, but it varies." Evans shrugged. "They

166

come and go, and lately they've been going fast, thanks to you."

"Where's the remuda?" Jessie asked. "What about cabins?"

Evans thumbed toward the canyon. "Tuther end, tuther side of that bend. Got a spring there, and a graze o' sorts, and a fenced corral. Only cabin worth a shake is Tode's adobe shack that's back thataway, too—to the left some and at path's end."

"If you're thinking of Augustas, Jessie, I doubt he's here."

"I was, Ki, and I agree. He can't have come and warned Tode. The camp's too calm."

"Well, let's catch 'em while they're still unaware," Renwick said. "Nine won't do to split up and surround 'em, so we'll hafta sneak down close and ring 'em from the sides as best as possible. If they won't surrender, we'll smoke 'em in crossfire."

The sheriff's orders, along with instructions on what to do in case of early discovery, were passed from man to man, for he did not wish to send them into a slaughter. Remaining dismounted, they took up reins and tugged their horses forward and down over the crest of the canyon. The minutes seemed to crawl, fraught as they were with danger while the posse descended. Except for Evans sticking to the sheriff, they fanned out individually to form a ragged crescent touching both canyon sides. They worked lower toward the campsite with horses muzzled, weapons cocked, ears tuned for any unusual sound, and eyes searching the rocks choked with wild timber and thorny growth.

Not far from Dwight Latimer, a berry shrub trembled slightly. The crown of a tall black hat appeared warily above it, as a roving sentry stabbed a suspicious glance about. Dwight turned to stone.

Across on the other bank, nearer Renwick and Evans, a

voice called hoarsely, "What's up, Harry? Y'see sumpthang o'er thar?"

"Heard something! Someone's around, damn it!" The hat quickly disappeared. A bird rose from the direction of the voice.

Sheriff Renwick shoved Evans back against his horse. "Mount up, pronto. Your pals have spotted us and they're movin' in!"

His words were hardly out of his mouth before Big Fletcher's carbine spat fire and lead from farther on. Another patrolling outlaw toppled from the eroded lip of an outcrop, rifle clattering. As if that were a signal for which everybody had been waiting, instantly the posse leaped asaddle, the other sentries opened up, and those in the camp scrambled, snatching their weapons.

Yelling like banshees, the posse launched into gallops and surged toward the canyon floor. Dwight recklessly threw his carbine to his shoulder, snapping a shot at the man he had glimpsed in the berry thicket, and he got an answering shout of pain. He grinned in satisfaction and scanned for a new target—as did the others, while at breakneck speed they converged on Tode's isolated and well-concealed lair. Jessie and Ki now more than ever appreciated that, without Arne Evans's help, they could have tracked these uplands for weeks before locating the outlaw camp.

They caught sight of Froggy Trode. There was no mistaking him as he came springing out of the black depths at the foot of a fluted scarp. For a moment he stood his ground there in the open, along with many of his henchmen who were bunched with rifles and revolvers flaming at the onrushing sweep of riders.

A searing pain sliced its way along the sheriff's forearm as a slug peeled the skin from his shoulder. Ignoring it and the lead streaking around, he stood in his stirrups and bellowed, "Drop 'em an' reach! Give up or go down in the name of the law!"

In response, the outlaws heightened their barrage while spreading toward the rocks and underbrush. The posse returned with volleys, and lead sang thick in the morning air.

Flinching from this deadly exchange, Arne Evans stridently bawled, "They'll wanna kill me first an' foremost! Loan me a gun!"

Sheriff Renwick wasn't sure Evans deserved much mercy or any trust. He took one of a brace of spare Colts stuck in his belt, however, and hurled it at Evans. "Catch! And point it right!"

Evans, snagging the .45, leaned and yelled, "Hey, Lou!" A running outlaw jerked around, and Evans plugged him in the brisket.

Spotting this, another outlaw cursed, "Damn snitch!" He fired his shotgun at Evans, who was among the riders coming on his right, wounding Evans with a splatter of buck. Ducking behind cover to reload, the man evidently glimpsed the same menace advancing on his left, for he shouted, "Crossfire, pards! They're hittin' in on both sides! Cut 'em off or we're skunked!"

His call stampeded his comrades, but it came too late. Already the flanking bushes and rocks were loud with riders. The air vibrated with the drumbeat of their whip-lashing gunfire.

Jessie picked off the shouter with a well-placed carbine shot. Unlike the rest of the posse, she and Ki were riding straight into the open center of the camp. Oblivious to the suicidal risk they were taking, they charged the racing outlaws, drawing their fire while heading directly through the canyon.

There was method to their seeming madness, though. For if Evans could be believed—and so far he'd been truthful—around the bend ahead was the gang's cavvy of horses. Sooner or later, they knew, the outlaws would stop defending and start retreating, scrambling to escape. So their mounts had better not be there.

"Hands up! Guns down!" Sheriff Renwick roared insistently, his foghorn voice piercing the din. "Surrender to the law, damn it!"

With blasting repeaters and superb horsemanship, the riders were trapping the outlaws in their campsite. Irresolutely one man tossed his spent revolver and raised his hands, squatting in hopes of not being hit. Two more saw him and followed suit, stunned by the firepower and swift encircling of the attack. But most of the outlaws continued fighting with desperate ferocity, determined to make a stand and well aware of the hangman that awaited their surrender.

Their fire blistered the posse, who twisted and turned furiously, trying to dodge the bullets as they closed in. They were not always successful, Jessie and Ki saw while pressing on. Brick Noone crawled with a broken leg away from his dead horse, which had rolled on him when it had fallen. Pops Shannon was shot and let out a horrified cry before tumbling face downward from his saddle. Another Nehalem hand lay with glassy eyes staring sightlessly at the sun. Dwight Latimer, his left arm hanging limp and bloody, spurred behind cover to thumb fresh loads awkwardly into his carbine.

Braving that lethal gunfire without faltering, Jessie and Ki swept past the camp, their horses' hooves scattering the blazing embers of the outlaw fire. And Arne Evans had not been lying.

Chapter 17

As Jessie and Ki rounded the canyon bend in churning dust and smoke, they caught sight of the remuda staked out on a spring-fed stretch of scrub timber and thatch grass. To the right was the fenced corral with a hay and tool shanty adjoining its far side; to the left was the path to Tode's adobe cabin. Jessie felt it beckoning her to follow.

Ahead, by the fringe of grass, Froggy Tode was slapping gear on the second of two roans. Turning, he stared for a disbelieving moment at the oncoming duo, then leaped for the other, fully saddled roan just as Jessie shot at him. Tode stumbled, Jessie's slug creasing his forehead, but he vaulted into stirrups and spurted toward the path to his cabin and, no doubt, to safety.

Levering, Jessie veered to cut him off. Her drive was longer, yet her speed was greater than his, and they verged on the gap in a virtual dead heat. Legs gripping her horse tightly, she used both hands to help steady and sight her carbine. Tode was aiming his revolver across at her, blood from the bullet gash dripping in eyes that bulged with malevolence—until they mirrored his alarmed realization that she had the advantage, and he frantically reined his horse away. The same instant Jessie triggered, and again a sudden move by Tode caused her to miss him.

Frustrated and swearing, Jessie crooked her carbine, retrieved her reins, and then guided her horse wheeling after. By then Tode had a lengthy gain on her and was heading directly back.

Ki, having ridden rearward to box Tode between him and Jessie, now maneuvered to block Tode's reversed flight. Tode glanced behind at the gun-toting woman and then thrust straight on at the apparently unarmed man. He likely would have in any event; his face was livid with the rage and rancor he harbored toward Ki, who had busted him in town and was to blame for spoiling matters ever since.

Confronting Tode, Ki was expressionless save for a thin-lipped, steely grin, though inwardly he also held a personal antagonism. This was to be a private dual. Moreover, Ki had sensed, just as Jessie had, a critical need to follow the path. For Tode had been readying two horses, and only one other of his breed would run out on his henchmen and leave them to die covering his getaway: Augustas.

"Don't help, Jessie. Take the path!" Ki shouted, gesturing. "I'll take care of it here and catch up! Take care, but take it!"

Jessie wasted no time on futile protests, despite her natural concern for Ki, despite her knowing Tode to be a tough, vicious, armed killer. She reined her horse around again, aware for reasons yet unclear that Ki truly wished her not to stay and that he felt the same urgent hunch as she about the path. She dived toward the gap, hearing Tode threaten Ki in a blustery sneer.

"I'll take care o' you here. Permanently! Kiss your slut bye-bye 'cause you'll hafta catch up with her in hell!"

Tode was plunging his roan straight at Ki, leveling his revolver and tripping its hammer. The bullet clipped Ki's vest where it swelled slightly from his hand thrusting inside, and a second wild shot past his ribs brought a cold laugh from between his teeth. The range was long, but his hand flashed out and moved with precision.

Two slim daggers speared Froggy Tode in the chest and dumped him from the saddle. His roan left him sprawled and twitching on the ground while it galloped onward, sideswiping Ki's dashing horse and swerving by on its snorting tear. Ki worked to check his horse, which jigged askew from the brush and was romping skittishly; then he swung it about, still dancing, and skidded to a halt. Dismounting, Ki ducked under the reins to go after Tode.

Tode was not where he had fallen, much to Ki's annoyance. The distance had been a shade too far, the daggers stabbing lethally, but not quite sinking deep enough to be instantly fatal. Tode was staggering on saggy legs away from Ki and toward the shelter of a rock clump some yards farther on. He fell to one knee, panting.

"Pack it in," Ki called. "Rest easy, Tode, you're through."

Tode turned, glaring, his face slick with sweat and his eyes dark with defiance. He had tenacious hold of his revolver, and as he aimed it, his voice rose rasping above the savage gunfire echoing from around the canyon bend. "I ain't done with this fight yet—or with you!" He triggered, his slug coming amazingly close.

A whirring *shuriken* pierced Tode and ripped a moan from him. He flung himself to the ground and began crawling. Ki sprinted to catch up, again yelling to surrender while Tode was just starting in along the edge of the rocks. Tode rolled over and pointed his smoking revolver. Another *shuriken* sliced into him, but he was beyond feeling or caring anymore, existing solely on pure hatred as he vainly tried to line his next shot. He was struck by two more *shuriken*, one slashing his arm, the other lancing into his right lower gut. The revolver dropped from his hand, but he did not pick it up. He was intent only on reaching cover, his right leg now hanging limp and useless as he dragged himself ahead. He died with his good knee crooked for the last shove that would have sent him all the way behind the rocks.

Ki went to make sure Tode had finally expired, then

swept up the revolver, and ran to his horse. Rarely had he seen such adamant stamina. He marveled at it as he rode to the remuda, but it reminded him of an old Japanese proverb that born murders require a lot of killing.

Circling the remuda to the spot farthest from the canyon bend, he tied his mount securely to scrubwood and began cutting the herd loose. The horses were stripped bare, for each man would keep his own gear; and they were mustangers, on the whole, too scrubby for workaday use, but perfect for his purpose. Then he returned to his spot, while the horses started drifting, cantankerous by nature and nervously agitated by the raging uproar and the scents of gunsmoke and blood.

"Hiiyah! Hiiyah!" Ki shouted, firing Tode's revolver skyward and yelling more. Alarmed, the horses began trotting away from him in the opposite direction, toward the canyon bend.

"Hiiyah!" Ki kept whooping and hollering and shooting after them, the horses quickening, ears flattening, nostrils flaring, and then galloping in earnest. They hit the bend in a snorting stampede.

Ki raced back to his own panicked horse as the camp abruptly erupted in howling, rattling confusion. He couldn't see the chaos, but while he was calming his horse, he listened and imagined the outlaws trying to catch their remuda before they were left stranded—the cussing and scrambling, windmilling arms and hats, perhaps some falling underhoof, and a few truly stupid ones turning gunfire from the posse onto the horses. And if he'd read those horses correctly, they'd ignore the madness and just rampage on through to freedom.

Chuckling, Ki mounted and headed toward the path, eager now to catch up with Jessie and hoping she had ridden into no danger.

* * *

Jessie had ridden as if her life depended on it. Her intuition insisted it did. Her reasoning confirmed it. The meaning of two horses being saddled had dawned on her—after thinking over every detail she could recall and knowing some strange fact must have alerted Ki.

So ever since Jessie had entered the gap, she'd been studying her surroundings, her ears straining to note the weakest noise. The gap proved to be merely a path until the hump of the first rise. Then it climbed to the right, while the path continued among baked stone slabs, through pockets of brush and cactus, and through slopes of stump growth and thickets. Any point might provide a spot for ambush, and she remained vigilant for anything, though the wilderness slumbered undisturbed with flitting insects and scratching little animals in the patches of sunlight.

The path had its share of blind curves. Reaching yet another, Jessie again paused to look around the curve as Ki had taught her to do. Two hundred yards beyond, she detected what she thought was a dim glow—as from a window and then seeping through a screen of tall, spindly desert growth. Using the field glasses from her bag, which she'd retrieved with the buckskin at the sanatorium, Jessie not only observed a lamplit window, but also discerned an adobe cabin. Tode's country estate.

Well, if she saw the window, the window could see her—which was why it was there, she figured. So Jessie angled off the path and, at a plodding walk, rode in a wide loop to approach the cabin from its backside and avoid that window. It took awhile, but finally she arrived at what appeared to be the last good thicket for cover before the cabin. Quietly dismounting, she tensed motionless, listening and scrutinizing the cabin and terrain.

Ahead and to her left, the cabin squatted in a flat clearing of stones and sage. Technically an adobe was a hut, she supposed, but this had the size of a cabin, bigger than a shack but smaller than a bungalow. Fleetingly she wondered who'd been the wild hermit who'd gone to such trouble building it here.

The side facing her had only one shuttered window. She couldn't see the opposite side, obviously, or the left end where the path-viewing window was. The right end was the front entrance with a ramshackle stoop and a warped door that canted rotten on its hinges. Of course, its hinges might be iron and a crossbar might be securing it, but Jessie refused to consider the possibilities at this point. Yonder the path came in and petered out between the door and a lean-to, where two horses stood with nodding heads. Two horses here plus one from Tode equal three riders. Dandy odds . . .

After anchoring her horse's reins under a rock, Jessie began to sneak carefully toward the cabin. She clung to what scanty shadow and puny growth she could find, and about midway there, feeling as exposed as a newborn babe, she considered perhaps she should've packed her carbine along. Gliding on, she decided she probably was better off without it.

Breathlessly she picked her way, gauging each footfall as though she were treading on eggs. When at last she reached the right rear corner of the cabin, she drew against it and listened while scanning the area. Then she darted across the open stretch to the lean-to and wedged between the horses. They shuffled to make room, nickering irritably from being shoved, but they were too logy from the growing heat to put up much protest.

Jessie crouched, drawing out her razor while she waited to see if anyone was attracted by the fuss. The horses fell quiet. Their cinches were loose as they should be if their riders had plans to stay awhile. Jessie made sure the cinches remained loose, by slicing off their leather buckle straps. There was also one carbine whose barrel she thoroughly plugged with dirt before replacing it.

Again she checked about, then crossed the open stretch, and faded along the back of the cabin. A few yards before the left corner, she located a round, palm-size rock. Then she eased out past the left end to where she could glimpse the path-viewing window.

Standing braced to run, Jessie heaved the rock at the window, and as she heard the crash and tinkle of shattering glass behind her, she sped along the side to the right end where the front entrance was. Still on the run, her shoulder smacked into the flimsy door and she burst into the lighted room without breaking her stride.

Three surprised men were grouped at the window, craning in search of the culprit who'd broken the glass and startled them. Still nervous from it, two of the three spasmed in shock as the door tore open in a wood-splintering, hinge-ripping, dust-geysering blast. Turning, they stared aghast at Jessie standing inside the doorway, her right hand confidently gripping the pistol that she was training on them.

They were strangers to Jessie. They were in their forties, she perceived, and dressed in eastern-style tailored business suits. The East—home of the moneymen and schemers behind the attempt to take over Rainbow Valley. And behind the moneymen and schemers was the cartel. A certain savage throb surged through Jessie as she savored her possible catch here. Maybe these two men are cartel agents, maybe it's merely coincidental. Well, the fish could all get sorted out later, she knew, but only after they'd all been netted and hauled in.

The third man was Augustas. He was another satisfying catch, though Jessie figured he deserved more to be harpooned than netted. Incredibly, despite his earlier route and panicky flight, Augustas was resplendent in pinstripe trousers, a frock coat, and a white shirt and vest. And having learned somewhere in his murky past to imitate a physician's dignified manner, Augustas was composed as he turned, sedately placing his hands in his frock coat and eyeing Jessie solemnly as though she were a recalcitrant child.

"The door has a latch on it," he said smoothly. *"Had* a latch. You could've opened it, Miss Starbuck. What do you want here?"

Jessie's eyes were ice-green as she swept the trio with her pistol. "I want you to drop your weapons and raise your hands."

One of the men bluffed, "But, but we do not—"

The click of Jessie's gun was loud and persuasive. Hastily the two men tossed aside .36 pocket-model pistols and lifted their hands. Augustas dumped a silvered .38 from a shoulder holster under his frock coat, then pocketed his hands again, and resumed his staid manner. "Now what do you want us to do?"

"Wait. Either your side or mine will show up."

"Ah." He beamed as if plump with a secret.

"Don't get too smug," Jessie said. "Tode may not show. If he does, I'll kill him like a skunk. If his gunmen show, I'll tell them how they got caught napping, that you and Tode kept news from them so they'd not turn on you or run out. You wanted to use them while you ran out—which you would've done by now, if Tode had arrived earlier with your horse." She turned to the other men. "Must've been a shock to come to a business meeting and find the business has been closed. But you've got contingency plans, don't you? You'll just move them safely to another region and set up shop again."

"Byron, how has she learned this?" one man demanded huffily. "Our affairs were to be kept in strictest confidence. Have you . . . ?"

"Dieter, she doesn't know a thing," Augustas growled, his composure slipping. "She's been a nuisance, a gadfly."

"No, Byron, she has ruined our operation here. Her name is Jessica Starbuck, *nein?*" The other man then gave

Jessie a nodding bow. "I am rewarded by your presence."

"Not as rewarded as you'd like to be," Jessie retorted, reminding him she knew of the price on her head. "But I'm not responsible for it. Augustas is: His greed, his butchery, ruined it."

Augustas was stung. "Hans, the woman is mad."

"I won't go into your cheating the sick and dying or killing local folks to grab this valley, because that's part of some master scheme and they're in on it," Jessie said disdainfully. "Planned murders, starting with killing Mr. Kessler to get his place for your san—"

"He is dead?" Dieter cut in and frowned at Augustas. "Then how could he demand the fat bonus you had us pay you to give him?"

"She's lying," Augustas snapped, his forehead perspiring.

Jessie resumed, "I will go into murders that aren't in the big scheme. Was Mr. Muldow poisoned for his estate? He was one of many, I venture, who signed a death certificate when writing you into a will. How long can you get away with that?"

"Byron, you know the rules! And so risky a sideline!"

"Hans, I'm not! I'm only working what we planned on." Augustas scowled at Jessie, his knuckles moving in his pockets. "Why are you doing this to me? I haven't done anything to you."

"You have. You killed Abram Volner because he recognized you from Dodge City," Jessie replied. "You killed a Starbuck man."

Dieter said, "Byron, I believe a review is needed."

Augustas quivered, fuming. "You take her word?"

Hans nodded. "She's Miss Starbuck. You'll have your say."

"It's beneath reply! There's nothing for me to say!"

"There's nothing to be said for you," Jessie countered.

Insane fury blazed in Augustas' eyes. Gone now was

the cloak he had assumed, and with a snarl he dug deeper into his coat pocket with his fingers—and the flat crack of a hidden derringer slashed through the cabin as he fired through the cloth.

A stinging arrow cut through Jessie's left thigh. Her leg collapsed beneath her and she fell to the floor on one knee.

Dieter and Hans, believing their cartel's enemy was out of the fight, dived for their pistols. With a cackling laugh, Augustas moved in for a second shot, the *coup de grâce*.

The cabin was filled with smoke and thunder as every pistol there erupted at the same instant. Hot lead searched both sides of the floor around Jessie as she stayed where she fell, her pistol clicking out vengeful death for the trio. Yet the only bullet taken during that first swift flurry was by Augustas. As he had advanced on Jessie with blood-thirsty confidence, her initial shot punched a hole in his gut.

Augustas floundered back against a chair by the broken window. He clung to it, wheezing and coughing, gathering his pain-ravaged strength. Everybody in that room—and he especially, having played doctor for so long—was aware that a man could live two or three days with a belly-shot like his. And as he straigthened, the gnarled expression on his face was as though he was determined that two or three days would be long enough for him to do what he had to do. Face contorted, eyes waxen with rage and agony, he lurched toward Jessie.

Dieter and Hans were at a disadvantage as Augustas staggered between them and Jessie on the floor. Jessie rose cautiously, her pistol ready, but she held her fire. She kept waiting for Augustas·to fall. Instead, his fingers twitched and he brought his derringer out of his coat pocket. Bringing the weapon up in front of him, he shoved it point-blank at Jessie. His thin lips rolled back from his teeth and he tried to speak, but no words came. His fingers tightened in a death grip on the trigger and moved it feebly.

Jessie fired in the nick of time. With a final, convulsive motion, Augustas pulled the trigger and the slug plowed through the floor at his feet. Jessie's shot drew blood through Augustas' frock coat—just over the heart. Augustas rocked from side to side, his feet planted wide apart to balance himself until, at last, he plunged to the floor. The sound of his fall was loud and hard in the stillness.

Shifting her aim hurriedly, Jessie covered Dieter and Hans. But for the moment, they had completely forgotten her presence, their eyes fastened on the lax form on the floor, fascination and horror on their faces. These two cartel men had been plotting wholesale murder schemes the way an accountant computes a budget, but they had never personally witnessed the kind of gory results their planning produced until this very instant. Death in its worst form was a ghastly portrait, and Jessie had seen stronger men than these get violently ill and even faint. Nevertheless, under the circumstances she felt nothing but contempt for them. Dieter and Hans were through. Their pistols thumped to the floor and they remained in frozen stances.

Moments later, Ki dashed inside, his eyes shining and his fingers poised on the weapons in his vest. But instantly he saw the fight was over, and he relaxed, looking almost a bit disappointed.

"Sorry I'm late, Jessie. I was circling and still had a ways to go when I heard the popping. I came as fast as I could."

"You're not late." She smiled serenely at Ki. "Everything was under control. I could use something like a neckerchief, though. I've one of those fair-size scratches that won't stop oozing for anything. My, those thorn thickets are treacherous."

Soon they set out on the path to return to the canyon. It was much quicker going this way than looping around, and now Jessie was sorry she had cut off those cinch straps. On the other hand, precaution is a smart move, and she'd have

181

been much sorrier if she hadn't cut them and found she should have. Besides, Dieter and Hans looked as though they were in need of a long, brisk walk.

When they dipped down out of the gap and headed toward the canyon bend, they realized how relatively quiet it was. The shooting was over. They could hear excited voices calling to one another, familiar voices like Norm Hodel's and Glenn Latimer's, and they smiled with relief and victory.

"It's all over," Ki told Jessie.

"Not quite. When we get back into the main canyon, I think I'll tell Glenn and Dwight the Box L is theirs. They've earned it."

"Be a good time for it, too, with the Nehalem crew there."

Then Sheriff Renwick's buffalo voice rose above the hubbub. "Mop up! Mop up, boys! Herd 'em all against the rock wall and make sure none keeps any souvenirs like knives and pistols!"

Jessie laughed. "Sounds like peace has come to Rainbow Valley at last, all right. I figure it's just what the doctor ordered."

Watch for

LONE STAR AND THE LAND BARONS

forty-eighth novel in the
exciting LONE STAR series, and

**LONGARM AND THE LONE STAR
SHOWDOWN**

a new giant LONGARM adventure
featuring the LONE STAR duo

coming from Jove in August!